No Game No Life 3
YUU KAMIYA
P9-DNV-399
ONE HALF OF THE GAMER SIBLINGS HAS DISAPPEARED!

If I take my eyes off Chlammy, why, she'll go crying in a corner, so I'd like to stay by her side.

"Fi...is my childhood friend. To be precise—my *master*, actually."

...Two,
in one...
Brother,
would...
never...
leave me,
alone...
—Shiro,
we are
always
two in
one.

Having lost her balance **dodging** the initial **barrage**—the one she aimed for was that "**Shiro**." There was **no** way she could miss, and the **clothes** that once served as a shield **remained hardly at all**.

"—Now it's getting fun, please!!"

Shiro had already lost her **uniform's coat** and **dress** and was down to her **shirt** and **knee-highs**.

Kannagari, capital of the Eastern Union—the **Inner Garden** of the **Central Division** of the **Shrine**.

"From **beyond** the **sea**, welcome to the **light of the spirit of the moon**."

THE TEN COVENANTS

The absolute law of this world, created by the god Tet upon winning the throne of the One True God. Covenants that have forbidden all war among the intelligent Ixseeds—namely.

1. In this world, all bodily injury, war, and plunder is forbidden.
2. All conflicts shall be settled by victory and defeat in games.
3. Games shall be played for wagers that each agrees are of equal value.
4. Insofar as it does not conflict with "3," any game or wager is permitted.
5. The party challenged shall have the right to determine the game.
6. Wagers sworn by the Covenants are absolutely binding.
7. For conflicts between groups, an agent plenipotentiary shall be established.
8. If cheating is discovered in a game, it shall be counted as a loss.
9. The above shall be absolute and immutable rules, in the name of the God.

10. Let's all have fun together.

YUU KAMIYA

NEW YORK

NO GAME NO LIFE, Volume 3
YUU KAMIYA

Translation by Daniel Komen

Yen On
1290 Avenue of the Americas
New York, NY 10104
www.yenpress.com

Yen On is an imprint of Yen Press, LLC.
The Yen On name and logo are trademarks of Yen Press, LLC.

The publisher is not responsible for websites (or their content) that are not owned by the publisher.

First Yen On Edition: October 2015

ISBN: 978-0-316-38519-0

10 9 8

LSC-C

Printed in the United States of America

LOADING

That first moment of self-realization. What does that even mean? If you're talking about oldest memories, though, hers was logged before the age of one. She didn't actually remember the first words she spoke. But the motherly woman who heard them, the pale face looking down at her—that was her earliest memory.

——……

Soon she was left in a white institution. A girl born too white in a building with white walls. Though there were other children there, she tried to blend into the background. Keeping her strangely ruby-red eyes cast ever downward. Always facing a stack of Western books—a decided mismatch with a little Japanese girl not yet even two years old.

…It was around then that she learned of games.

The white-clad grown-ups brought out all these games they called "intelligence tests." But they were all too simple, too boring. No fun to play with anyone—these games. With only the word *unmeasurable* left behind, after a while there was no one who would play with her. After about a year in the institution, she realized it was more tolerable to play by herself. As the little girl continued playing both sides, in chess, shogi, go, etc., she blended into the background. Eventually, not even the white-clad adults tried to talk to her.

...Silent, stark-white memories.

A series of memories labeled simply: *boring*—

After two years, the woman who was apparently her mother came again. In the girl's memory, the woman told her excitedly that she would have a new father, but the eyes with which the woman faced her were the same as those of the white-clad grown-ups of the white institution—an empty gaze from which could be gleaned nothing. By this time, she was three. The girl met some man called her "new father" and his son—a *boy* seven years older. A boy who gave calculated answers as the *grown-ups* talked, calculated smiles. All alone, the boy returned exactly what he was given. To this boy who distributed *empty, inorganic smiles*, she opened her mouth that had long been closed.

"...You really, are...'empty'..."

—The boy who'd given his name as *Sora*, which meant *Sky* or *Empty*, opened his eyes wide at the words the girl muttered. He stared fixedly into the girl's red eyes, with which no one had wanted to make contact. Looking for something, trying to check something silently, it seemed...and then she remembered—a *color* she had never seen before appearing in his face. At the time, she had no way of understanding the meaning behind that color. The boy—*Sora*—spoke.

"Come on, let's play a game."

—That day, for the first time, the girl found a game *fun*.

They played twenty times. The first few times, the girl destroyed him utterly. But, as they played on, gradually, his moves became harder to read. Leading her on and tricking her with moves that sneered at common sense, starting to make moves so out there she never would have imagined them, *Sora* flew far beyond her comprehension to victory and in the end earned a 10-to-10 draw. The boy who had defeated her for the first time, yet without posing or gloating. Rather, it was as if he was the one who had lost—and as if *he was giddy with joy at that*. There was no more emptiness in his face. His face a color the true meaning of which she still did not understand, the boy—Sora—her *brother* spoke.

"Sorry to be a no-good brother who can only win by sneaky tricks, but I hope we can get along—*Shiro [White]*."

The color in his face— The girl who felt as if her name had been spoken for the first time, she realized it was the *love of family* and that she was *wanted*, for the first time. Understood that it was all right for her to be here, that she was recognized and accepted.

—Her inorganic, monochrome memories clearly changed at this time to have color. She felt something hot welling up in her heart, but she didn't know yet what it was. All she could do was to drop her gaze and nod subtly.

——……

…Time flowed on, and it came to be that the *brother* and *sister* lived together by themselves. The two who had called themselves their parents were already gone.

"Well, I guess this means we'll stay together from now on, too."

This one statement from the mouth of her brother was all the girl wanted. It was around then that they started playing online games under a single name. An account registered under a string of two spaces, from what their names spelled written together: *Kuuhaku [Blank]*. The brother would devise his outlandish, bizarre strategies that the sister never would have thought of, while the sister implemented his tactics far beyond his imagination with the accuracy and calculation of a precision machine.

—This was the time the "two-in-one gamer" clearly emerged. The time when this gamer won victory after victory, beyond belief, and began to be whispered of online as an urban legend.

* * *

—Then began her memories that she herself could hardly believe. Beating someone who called themselves a god at online chess, and then—being dumped into another world. Where violence was forbidden by the Ten Covenants and everything was decided by games: *Disboard.*

How would you normally feel when suddenly thrown into another world? Nervous, lonely, displaced...? But her memories recorded not one of these emotions. From the beginning, her place could be only in her brother's arms. Together with her brother, she challenged the world where everything was decided by games.

—Oh, how perfect. What more could one ask—?

■■■

"I got it...all I have to do is become female!"

A voice rang through the Presence Chamber of the Royal Castle in Elkia, capital of the Kingdom of Elkia. It belonged to the young man with disheveled black hair sitting on the throne—Sora. Wearing a T-shirt that said "I ♥ PPL" and the queen's tiara twisted around his bicep like an armband to indicate that, here in this world, Disboard, he was the king of Elkia...and of Immanity. Turning suspicious gazes at the king's sudden pronouncement were three.

"...Whatever is His Royal Highness yapping about now?"

One with red hair, contrasting with her icy blue gaze. Stephanie Dola, aka Steph. The granddaughter of the previous king of the Kingdom of Elkia, a girl with an air that suggested the quality of her upbringing. But in this case, the expression she had turned on Sora was unexpected.

"—I see, my master indeed is wise; what a profound revelation."

Another, praising Sora's pronouncement with a hot amber gaze. Jibril—a girl as beautiful as a fantasy, with long hair that refracted light and changed its color. The wings from her hips and the halo revolving above her head showed that she was not human, but Flügel. She, one of Rank Six of the intelligent Ixseeds of this world, accepted this wisdom from her master—one of Rank Sixteen, Immanity, the lowest of the Ixseeds—clasping her hands together as if contemplating divine word, and she extracted his intent.

"You mean that, if you yourself were female, Master, all adult situations could be written off as mere 'Eek! Tee-hee-hee!' among intimate members of the same sex… I am overcome with emotion at your insight."

Sora, nodding, *mm-hmm, mm-hmm*, contentedly, made eye contact with the last one.

"Come—my sister! Let us play a game under *Aschente*! And please defeat me!"

The girl Sora called his sister, the girl on his lap with ruby eyes—Shiro. The eleven-year-old whose long hair as white as snow was tied with the king's crown. King Sora's sister—that is, Queen Shiro—peered into the brother's eyes and mumbled.

"…I, don't think…you, can."

"Huh, why not? Wagers sworn by the Ten Covenants are absolutely binding, right? I forced Steph to fall in love with me and made Jibril my property. So I should be able to become female, too, right?"

"Could you please not gloss over all your heinous deeds as if they were nothing?!"

Though Steph screamed piteously—souls so gentle as to pay attention to her were absent.

"—Even so, Master, I'm afraid Her Majesty's point is valid."

"Huh, why?"

"It is because *theoretically impossible demands cannot be carried out.*"

As Shiro nodded at Jibril's words, Sora finally understood.

…Oh. It was obvious once you thought about it.

"So, like, if I were to beat Steph with the condition, 'Run a hundred meters in one second,' it's still physically impossible, and she could only run as fast as she could to do her best to obey the demand."

"Exactly, my lord."

"—Um… Why are you using me as an example?"

Imagining herself forced to run like a madwoman in a suicidal attempt to run a hundred meters in one second. Steph interrupted with apparent trepidation that Sora might actually try this.

"Wait a sec, then does that mean even if I played a game that required me to get a life, I still couldn't?!"

Sora imagined what he would look like with a life.

—How about that? He could hardly come up with anything but fantasies far removed from reality.

"Whether or not you could actually 'get a life,' as you put it, you should most likely be able to feel as though you have. After all, you speak of issues of your personality, which in the end is a mere abstract conception."

"A shut-in loser game vegetable who thinks he has a life—that's just too horrible to contemplate!!" Sora shrieked despairingly as he tried to picture it.

"…I guess I'd better check the limits of the covenant constraints…"

As he started pondering more seriously than ever, Steph gave him a squinting look to say, "Work." Meanwhile, Shiro, who had lost herself in thought just like her brother, proposed an experiment.

"…Try…a personality change…with, some conditions?"

"Hmm, that would make it easy to see. 'Kay, Steph, let's do this."

"—Um, let me ask one more time. Why does it have to be me?"

"Because you're the best if we want to check how far we can go."

Sora's goal as he casually dropped what passed for an explanation was still incomprehensible to Steph.

"Come, let's start the game. The wager—is that Steph become me."

—

"……All right, fine."

Steph, repressing the emotion she was on the brink of revealing and answering instead with a resigned *act*.

…Yes, she would probably lose to Sora no matter what she did. After all, that had consistently been the case—in fact, she still hadn't a clue how she could win a game against him. Besides, this was an experiment, so she'd have to lose intentionally. But if the result, albeit qualified, was that *she could become Sora*—? (Could this be...my one and only chance to beat him?!) Desperately hiding the dark *heh-heh-heh-heh* that threatened to spill out of her heart...

"There's just no arguing with you... All I need to do is lose intentionally, right?"

"I mean, you're gonna lose whether you try or not. Anyway, this is an experiment, so let's make the conditions clear... The game is chess. If I win, Steph becomes Sora for thirty minutes. For the sake of argument, if Steph wins, we'll say I'll give her a candy. Not that it makes any difference. So—*Aschente*."

"Yes, *Aschente...hfff*."

Even the storm of verbal abuse was tolerable to Steph when she considered what might come *after she lost*.

—Making the oath of *Aschente*: a declaration that one submitted to an absolutely binding wager under the Ten Covenants set forth by the God—

——......Forty seconds later.

"...Steph, can you really suck this much? That's hard to do even intentionally..."

Though Steph lost in a mere five moves, still she answered Sora's insult with a smile.

"Heh-heh-heh...noww, this means that *there is one more greatest gamer among Immanity*—"

Steph, her eyes suddenly piercing as she sported a crookedly ironic grin, taunted gleefully.

"C'mon, let's play us a game, 'Sora'—it's time for you to face *yourself*, bitch, the one who claims he's gonna take down the God himself!"

The girl's condescending tone was incongruous with the finery in which she was adorned.

"Heh-heh, what's wrong? Leery of leaping into the grave you dug yourself? The wager is that you be a decent person permanently, bitch. Come—let's get this '*Aschente*' on!"

Such was the pretentious manner in which Steph (in the style of Sora, allowing for some degree of error) carried herself.

—Striking poses with each punctuation. At this display:

"Hey, Shiro, am I this kind of character?"

"...It's...pretty, off."

"Dora is probably doing her best to fulfill the covenant, based on her view of you, Master."

Oh, trying to act as if she had a—not a life, as if she were Sora.

"...It's hard to tell whether she's overestimating me or making fun of me..."

Watching Steph dandily sweep at her bangs and wondering, *Have I ever actually done that?* Sora, with a strained expression, halfheartedly answered her challenge.

"...Uh, okay, whatever. It is creepier than I thought, so I'm gonna demand that you turn back to Steph right now—*Aschente*."

——......Another forty seconds later.

"Whyyy?! I thought I was going to become your equal in skill?!"

...To Steph, beaten as always, Jibril replied, as naturally as the flow of a river.

"What? I thought I explained that *things that are physically impossible cannot be done*."

"It's physically impossible for me to beat Sora?!"

The face of one betrayed by the world: Truly, that must have been as Steph's visage now.

"You see, little Dora, even if you *intend* to be Master, you still cannot share his thoughts or memories."

"Y-you knew this before you accepted the match, didn't you?!"

"Of course I did! Look back at yourself. What makes you think you looked equal?!"

—To begin with, if she had actually become Sora, she alone, without Shiro, would never have boasted the title of greatest among humans.

"Hngg... But I'm still not clear on this. It could have just been Steph's insufficient specs."

"Could you not say I have insufficient specs?!"

"Jibril, let's try it with you. A Flügel should be able to emulate me, right?"

The physical specs of Flügel were literally in a whole different dimension from those of Immanity. Could it be—? Sora prayed, but unexpectedly Jibril seemed surprised.

"You suggest that I become you? I believe that may yet be impossible."

"Huh, why?"

"...Well, if it is your wish, Master, I shall stake all my spirits to attempt it."

With a look of some kind of frightening resolve, Jibril lowered her head.

——......Jibril, having lost intentionally as agreed. Bound absolutely by the Covenants—started to transform.

"Whoa?! You transform!"

"...I, see...Jib-ril...is, composed...of, spirits..."

Sora and Shiro together widened their eyes and raised their voices. Huh. So for a Flügel, changing one's appearance was *not theoretically impossible*! This was a result that held out a thread of hope for the Sora Sex Change Project which had all but plunged into despair—Sora's face melted with glee but then gradually stiffened. Jibril transforming to look like Sora, like a mirror—that was all right. But, gradually—*sprouting eight wings.*

"...E-eh?"

An enormous halo even more complex than Jibril's original one was drawn over her head. And her mouth, opening gently—formed words.

"—I am: the most powerful."

...Not only Sora, but everyone, including Shiro and Steph, was dumbstruck.

"U-umm...?!"

"The weakest and yet the most powerful: I am he who shall rise against the God and unite the Ixseeds. I am he who redefines the old knowledge as ignorance—and therefore I am he who shall reign over the reformation of the world… What business have ye with me, ye powerless creatures?"

—And a long hush fell over them.

"Uuuuumm—"

So this is what it meant.

"So Jibril is overestimating me with heaven-busting force…"

It was as Jibril had said, after all: Being unable to share his memories meant that subjective perceptions would inevitably enter.

—Well anyway, Jibril had identified him as the new lord she should serve, on an equal footing with her creator. It made sense that Jibril would see Sora as some kind of god—but.

"Hey, am I really this much of a dweeb?"

"…Uh? Kind, of…"

"It is a bit of a caricature, but it does more or less accurately portray Sora's behavior, doesn't it?"

As Shiro and Steph responded to his question as if it were even more surprising than Jibril's transformation, Sora considered.

"…Maybe I should seriously reevaluate myself."

Looking as if he literally wanted to crawl into a hole. Sora decided to cover his face with his hands and erase Jibril's subjective portrayal of him from his vision.

——……

"…So basically, even the absolute binding power of the Covenants is unable to push people past their limits."

To Sora reaching this conclusion with a heavy sigh, Jibril, once more herself, replied:

"I'm afraid so, Master. So for you to become female—"

"—ah…regrettably, it is impossible."

But that was only natural.

"Yeah…if we could enforce things that went beyond the limits and abilities of the people involved in the game, then indirectly it would be possible to give Immanity powers like magic."

But Sora, continuing with a "Really—"

"*That's what I was hoping for*—but I guess it's not so easy to find a loophole in the rules."

"—!"

His announcement made Steph and even Jibril gasp. He was looking (however frivolously)—*for a loophole in the absolute and immutable rules of the world* set forth by the One True God.

—That was Sora—the king of Immanity. The one Jibril had decided to serve. But it didn't appear Sora himself was conscious of it. While Steph and Jibril stood stunned, it seemed only Shiro was used to it as "how her brother was." To Shiro, as if he'd already moved on, Sora slowly introduced a different proposal.

"All right, so we'll say you can't force anything, but Shiro—can you make me 'Shiro'?"

Shiro cocking her head.

"...What, for?"

"Well, I've always been curious about how you see the world."

"...You'll, just, be...the, Shiro, you perceive...just like, with the other, two."

"Sure, but still, then I'll have the binding power of the Covenants on my side. I just thought if I could max out this emulation to a level not normally achievable, maybe I'd see a little something new."

But her brother's words made Shiro think.

—Her brother was definitely not as dumb as he thought he was. In fact, he had beaten her any number of times with wily tricks she would never have thought of. Shiro could hardly imagine why her brother would call himself dumb. The one thing you could say... was that he was, well—kind of *dense* in some weird ways. What if the power of the Covenants enabled Sora to get over that denseness? Given that Sora had lived the same time the same way Shiro had ever since that day they met and that the two shared much the same memories. Would he still fail to notice? *Her feelings.*

—The feelings hidden in her heart, for her brother, as *more than a brother.*

* * *

Thinking this, what Shiro said was a move to block off her brother's request completely. Divergent from her true motive; soft, yet closing the path with knockout force—an excuse.

"...Brother...what, would you think...if I, became...you?"

"—Oh. Yeah, that would suck. To find out how you really see me, in the worst-case scenario, could kill me."

—It did after all keep her brother from noticing. Though his sister's cheeks went faintly red...the significance escaped his notice.

"Hmm... Okay then, Jibril, wanna be Steph?"

"I don't mean to argue, Master, but I fail to see the purpose in increasing the number of comic relief characters."

"Who are you calling a comic relief character?!"

—Shiro's life, which had started in monochrome. Shiro now understood what had welled up in her heart that time, but she remained unused to expressing it. She smiled too subtly for most people to notice. But her brother couldn't fail to see. Sora subtly smiled back, and the meaning in his eyes came through clearer than words.

—"This is fun." This world—this situation in which they could play games with a smile. Or the fact that Shiro was smiling. Not needing to clarify which, as her brother's eyes told her that it was both, Shiro nodded subtly—

—and then everything went black.

■■■

Her eyelids were heavy. Her eyes, terribly dry as if she'd been crying in her sleep, were so heavy that they refused to open. No, maybe it was because they were dry... She was reminded of a nightmare she didn't want to think about, didn't even want to imagine. Don't check whether it's real or a nightmare, don't open your eyes to see what lies before them—it felt to Shiro as though someone somewhere in her head was thus refusing. But, in order to deny this. In order to assert that it was impossible. She shut up the thoughts that demanded she stop, and with some actual pain, she narrowly opened her eyes. It was the royal bedchamber of the Elkia Royal Castle. Lying on a bed so huge one had to wonder just how many people were supposed to sleep there was Shiro alone. The room had countless games strewn about and a mountain of books—and that was all. No matter how many times she looked around, the one who should have been there...wasn't. The one who would have greeted her with *good morning* and given her a reason to live today.

—Sora wasn't there—in the lonely room. The implication of that... Her thoughts trying to deny it seemed to whisper.

—"I told you."

"...Please...if, this is a dream——end!"

With a sound she rarely made, squeezed shrill and scratchy enough to hurt, she shrieked.

—The empty room telling her that all these memories were but an illusion. She only choked back a sob and shrieked.

CHAPTER 1 SKY WALK

DISSOCIATION

Three moves remain

—I have no awareness or memory or senses. Where am I. Who am I. Such questions no longer arise. I don't feel anything. What do I ask when the very definition of myself has become unclear? I can't ask anything. I have no basis to ask anything. At best I suppose I can ask what to ask. My consciousness dims, near void, but that consciousness feebly, powerfully asserts. Without any evidence, just: "Everything is all right." Its assertion that all I have to do is *wait here for victory* is all that connects me to what remains of my sanity.

—Victory? At what?

—I don't know… I don't know anything.

"…How…is she?"

In front of the royal bedchamber, Steph put the question to Jibril. But Jibril only sighed again and shook her head.

"—Nothing. She refuses to admit me; I am at a loss."

"She still only repeats 'Sora' endlessly?"

"Yes...and what about you?"

"I asked whomever I could find among the staff within the castle. They all gave the same answer—"

"That *they know no one named Sora*; the only monarch of Elkia is Master—I suppose?"

"Yes...what does it mean?"

"That's what I want to know," sighed Jibril once more.

"The most natural conclusion would be that *Master's memories have been rewritten*, but..."

"But that—"

"Yes. It would mean that Master—*lost*."

—Something felt so very not right. Shiro having suddenly lost herself and calling for some unknown person named Sora over and over, in a stupor. The situation itself was more than perplexing, but it was *something even more not right* that made them frown.

—Perhaps she had heard their conversation. A thin, flat object slid under the door.

"...? Is this...?"

"Yes, it is Master's tablet."

Picking it up from the floor, Jibril and Steph looked at the screen together.

"It is in the language of Master's old world—it reads, 'Questions.'"

Pwok, a noise went. A new message appeared.

"I see. This is a window into, not an exchange of letters, but a *chat*."

The vast store of knowledge her master had brought from another world. Even Jibril had not yet been able to grasp it in its entirety, but she got the point.

"What does it say now?"

Steph, peering into the screen but in the end being unable to make heads or tails of it.

"—'1. What is the name of the person who played against Jibril?' "

"...It's...Shiro, isn't it?"

"Indeed. So...how do we—?"

Though Jibril failed to understand how to operate the technology, another *pwok* came straightaway.

"I see, so we may answer orally—'2. Who demanded that Steph fall in love?' "

"I-it's Shiro, I say."

Immediately, the next message came.

"...Well, it says...'3. An eleven-year-old girl demanded that you fall in love with her?' "

"Y-yes... I-isn't that why I have been excoriating you as a pervert and a monster...?"

Her strained answer and the following message arrived at the same time.

"—It says...'4. How did you lose, in detail?' "

Steph said that, considering Shiro's situation, she couldn't give a glib answer. Trying to remember in as much detail as she could, she placed her fingers on her forehead and thought hard.

"Umm, it was rock-paper-scissors. You challenged me to a psychological standoff, going for a draw. But the key point was the demands; you gave vague conditions in the case of a draw and took advantage. I protested that that was fraud, but you ignored me and told me...to fall in love with you."

At the same time as Steph finished, the next message arrived.

"—'5. Why did I demand that you fall in love with me instead of becoming my possession?' "

"S-so I would fall at your feet. But then you realized you made a mistake and were moaning and groaning about it—*Shiro*."

This time it was a while before the next message popped up.

"—'6. Who uncovered the game of the Eastern Union?' "

On this point, both Steph and Jibril concurred.

"It was you, Shiro, with the legacy of my grandfather."

"That matches my recollection."

...And then the next message did not come. Steph and Jibril, with no option but to wait silently, remained standing in front of the royal bedchamber. Perhaps few minutes later. But no longer even a question—a statement. More precisely…a plea, a declaration seemingly devoid of conviction.

`Your memories must have been erased.`

To this message, Jibril replied.

"Master, if I may, *the holder of rights to memories is the one who possesses them.* This 'Sora' could have played a game for his own memories, but it would be impossible to erase someone else's."

But a counterargument came without pause.

"All consented to the wager."

"—In such a case, it would be difficult to explain why *only you, Master, still kept your memories.*"

…Once more, no response forthcoming. Beyond the door sat Shiro, phone in hand, face buried in her lap, unable to answer.

—She knew. Would her brother have played a game without her? A game with a potential outcome like this, and on top of that *lost*—

"Uh, oh, yes. Your service is appreciated… No, it's no great matter."

From outside the door came Steph's voice faintly.

"…Shiro, this is difficult to say, but the messenger I sent just returned. Protests have been going on about your single-handed wager of the Immanity Piece, and we weren't able to hear what they were saying from within the castle, but apparently the target of the crowd's rebuke—does not include the name Sora."

Shiro feeling at this report her vision dimming once again. Gritting her teeth so as not to let go of her consciousness, she thought: There should be. Some contradiction in their memories. There had to be. Since, after all—

—if that were not the case, it would mean that *all her memories were false.* (Im-possible…it's not…ac-ceptable!) Shiro, insisting to herself, shaking her head desperately in denial. She'd lost in a game, and false memories had been planted in her—hypothetically, hypothetically, let's suppose that. But could *someone from this world* have managed to fabricate all those memories of the world she used to live in? That was too much; no one should have been able to do that. She tried to convince herself, but still Shiro knew—it was debatable. This world had *Covenants* and *magic*. It could be that they hadn't altered her memories specifically, but for example... *Split all her memories in two*, perhaps.

—No, to be more precise. Given that now she had no proof whatsoever of her brother's existence. Who was to say that she was sane? Considering just how convenient it was for her for this Sora to exist... This possibility—this most unacceptable of possibilities—came into fearfully persuasive relief. That is—that *Sora was just a convenient fiction she had dreamed up*. (—I, won't...accept, that...I, can't accept that!) There was no way she could accept it. If she did, everything about her—from the very foundation—

The tablet completely ceased to respond. Shiro's low state was palpable through the door, and Steph and Jibril looked at each other.

"Wh-what does it mean? What should we do?!"

"...Let's collect our thoughts."

Jibril spoke as if to calm herself.

"Right now, on the eve of a game with the Eastern Union betting the Immanity Piece—wagering for all of Immanity's rights—who stands to gain the most from incapacitating Master?"

"Even I can see that—the culprit is the Eastern Union, is it not?!"

—Indeed: That the Eastern Union, having had its game exposed, had challenged Shiro in secret before the official match, rendered her irrecoverable and wiped memories—that was the most natural conclusion. But looking at the log of the messages from Shiro, Jibril considered.

> *—6. Who uncovered the game of the Eastern Union?*

"...If it was the Eastern Union, they should have erased *this memory* first."

The Eastern Union, for many years, had concealed their game by demanding the erasure of memories pertaining to it. It was because their secret was uncovered that they were forced to take up the match—to say nothing of the fact that:

"Master would have had no reason to accept the challenge."

The Ten Covenants: The party challenged shall have the right to determine the game. Of course, that included whether to accept a challenge at all. It was hard to think of a reason to accept a match proposed by the Eastern Union...

"—Alas, it is a dead end... We simply have not nearly enough information to explain this situation."

Jibril, shaking her head, sighed with an expression dark with distress. From inside the room came only Shiro's sobs, as if about to cough blood. Before her liege lady who could only keep calling for her brother—a man named Sora—Jibril was compelled to act.

—Certainly she could not *doubt* her lady. Should her lady say that crows were white, it would be her duty to travel three thousand worlds coloring every crow thusly. Therefore, if her lord said that a person named Sora existed, he existed without a doubt. But the voice audible beyond the door—

"C-can't we do anything?! At this rate, Shiro isn't going to *last*!"

It was enough to make Steph dig her nails into the door in vexation and scream.

—Ixseed Rank Six, Flügel: a war race with vast spirit—magical power. Their very essence was a kind of "complete magic" woven by gods, and as a result, they were unable to use complex magic. Furthermore, they lacked complex emotions so as to be able to fully grasp the subtleties of the heart of Immanity. But.

"...That does...seem...to be the case."

—Even without using the likes of magic, it was plain that her lady's psyche was *one step away from collapse*. Certainly she could not doubt her lady. Doing so would deserve ten thousand deaths. Yet—

"—Master. Let us play a game."

"...Huh?"

Steph was startled by Jibril's suggestion—as was Shiro behind the door.

"Will you play an *Aschente* game with me? And—I am aware this is most impertinent, but—will you please lose?"

—The sobs didn't stop. But sensing that Shiro was groping for her intent, Jibril elaborated.

"I shall demand that all your memories concerning Sora be sealed."

At the Flügel's pronouncement, Steph's eyes bulged. The meaning of her gaze was clear even to Jibril. She must have had the same sense that something was *not right*. Jibril had the vague impression that it was *not right* to cut down Shiro's assertions—but.

"At this rate, Master will—break down."

That had to be avoided above all, even if it meant accepting ten thousand deaths. Under normal circumstances, what they should have done was figure out the covenant that had been exchanged and act to disable it. But it was self-evident that should they take time for such measures, Shiro would break first. They would seal her memories first, then calm her and track down the culprit, and then—*I swear I shall chop off their heads on the spot and mince them to dust.* As Jibril lost all traces of her usual mild smile and came to exude only a piercing, weighty *malice*, Steph, all but petrified, tried feebly to chastise her.

"Ji-Jibril, p-please calm—"

But Jibril's aura allowed no further discussion.

—The Ten Covenants forbade violence…*so what?* She could just track down the culprits, challenge them to a game, force them to grant her permission to kill them, and subsequently murder them with her own hands. After that, she could bow her head to any kind of punishment for doubting her lord. *Booop*, chimed an alert as an app started up on the tablet in Jibril's hands. Shiro, from her phone, had remotely launched—a shogi app. A finite, zero-sum, two-player game with perfect information, the sort in which Shiro had not a chance in a million of losing. Therefore—had she the intention of losing, *she could do so with certainty.* A paper-thin voice discernable between sobs reached Jibril's ears.

"…*A-sche…n…te…*"

With a deep bow, the Flügel responded.
"I thank you, my master...*Aschente.*"

■■■

Four moves remain

—I have no memory; I don't even know who I am. My arms have already lost all feeling. I hear voices, but I don't know whose they are. Who in the world am I, and why am I here? Why am I playing this game? Everything is hazy, but even so... If everything else falls into oblivion, one core precept still prods me forward. I absolutely cannot lose. Given the situation with my arms, I pick up a piece with my mouth. Deciphering the numerals on the pieces with my tongue, I select one. Don't think about what it means. It doesn't matter what it means. *We don't lose.* **That's right—...doesn't lose.**
—Who doesn't lose?

...No, don't think about it; it doesn't matter! On my shoulder—the warmth of someone's hand. Don't doubt the little feeling remaining that says this is the answer to everything. As my mind starts to go, sweeping away the madness—or perhaps entrusting myself to it—I place the piece in my mouth on the board.

■■■

—Pure, straightforward shogi. A game Shiro could easily bring to victory...or likewise to defeat. Indeed, it was simple. All she had to do was let Jibril take her gold general now, and that would be the end. That would mean her unceremonious defeat, and all of it would be sealed away. All the memories she'd shared with her brother. Her time with him, the first person who made her feel alive. Who told her she looked cute when she put on her uniform for the first time. Who held and cried with her after she got home from the entrance ceremony at the school she would never attend again. The one who took a girl incapable of doing anything by herself and gently led her by the hand. Her brother… Brother, who was more important to her than anyone— With a single move, it would be as if their time together had never happened. —…*!* The memories, the words of a brother who might have been a fabrication, cascaded through her mind. Without even thinking, Shiro moved her hand.

Jibril closed her eyes and whispered.

"…Master, why…must you *win*?"

Yes—a move trapping her opponent so deftly one couldn't even laughing call it *unbeatably*. The voice that answered Jibril's question was all too feeble. Yet with a force sufficient to push Jibril and Steph a step away from the door, it resounded:

"…Blank…doesn't—lose!"

Shiro's chest heaving in the dark, isolated room. Her face tear-stained as she clawed at her blankets, her only thoughts of her brother. His words to her that day she'd come home sobbing after her one and only day at school.

—Hey, Shiro. They say people can change, but is that really true? If you wish with all your might to be able to fly, can you sprout wings? I don't think so. Maybe what needs to change isn't *you*, but your *approach*. You have to create it—a *way to fly just as you are*. You've got to come up with one. I guess you're wondering what I'm talking about when I can't fly myself, but let's try to come up with some wings that'll let you fly… We'll take our time. I know I'm a no-good brother, but I'll try to help you think of something, 'kay?

—If she forgot this, how could she live? If she sealed away her memories of her brother—the very reason she could live in the first place—what else was there? If these were planted memories, what kind of brutal match had she accepted? 'Cause this—this—was too much!

"...Brotherrr...nooo...I don't want, to forget Brother—I'd much rather die!!"

At that voice which sounded every bit as if it might tear out their master's throat, neither Jibril nor Steph could do anything but gasp.

...A proposal on pain of ten thousand deaths. Having had it rejected, there was now nothing Jibril could say. Stepping past the defeated Flügel, whose eyes were now fixed on the floor, Steph reluctantly opened her mouth.

"U-um...I-I can't claim to understand the situation well, but..."

It wasn't logic prompting Steph's remarks. They were merely the articulation of her vague yet heartfelt desire—to console Shiro.

"For you, Shiro...Sora definitely existed, right? So without him, you come to this. You have no room for doubt—so definitely."

—But Steph's remarks...

"If that's the case, then this Sora person must have had a *reason for creating this situation*, right?"

—Steph's remarks shattered assumptions and brought in one ray of hope. Yet of the three collected there, she was the only one who didn't realize it. As if time had stopped, both Jibril and Shiro's eyes went wide, and they froze.

"H-however, is it not true that this situation cannot be explained by erasure of memory by the Cove—"

"Oh, that...I mean, that's not—seee..."

Steph's next suggestion was the one that stole their breath.

"—Could it be...*the game has yet to conclude*?"

Jibril's eyes as round as glass beads. Unable to grasp the meaning behind her gaze, Steph stammered.

"Y-you see—could it not be that what is rewriting our memories is not the Covenants, but *the game itself.* And if we assume Shiro is correct that hers are not the memories that have been rewritten, but *ours*...then, well...that could mean that this 'Sora' attained our consent for s-such a game, and it's...still not...over...or something..."

As Steph's confidence failed and her words trailed off, Shiro raised her wet face.

"—Wh-what basis do you have...?"

Jibril wrung her hands as she wrestled with this hypothesis, which seemed to leap out of nowhere in absurd disregard for the evidence present.

"B-basis...? I—I just feel it's *wrong*."

No, Steph had no evidence—*and that was why.* Words elicited by emotion rather than intellect just spilled out of her.

"*This person*—could not conceivably lose."

This person—a neutral designation specifying neither *Shiro* nor *Sora*—made Jibril close her mouth.

—Steph's hypothesis was full of holes. It was unclear how such an alteration of reality could be possible without the Covenants. And what purpose would be served by leaving only the agent plenipotentiary—Shiro—with memories of this specific person while erasing them from everyone else? Should Steph's supposition prove true, though, there was no question it would explain any number of the thornier issues now vexing them.

—The monarch of Elkia, the monarch of Immanity, her own lord. Who had brought down a god, who had brought down a Flügel—who intended to swallow up the Eastern Union! For this person to *lose*? The very notion felt...*not right.*

What if Steph's hypothesis was correct and this inscrutable situation *had not been orchestrated by the enemy* at all but was rather *a scenario designed to achieve victory*—?

"In that case, there is a way in which we can confirm."

Jibril nodded her head and elaborated.

"It is true that, even using the Covenants, it would be impossible to erase from all memories and records in the world the fact that a specific object or individual existed. However, if we suppose—"

The conditions demanded by this hypothetical scenario were quite severe. Accomplishing it *without the power of the Covenants* only deepened the mystery—and yet.

"—that a person named Sora was Master's brother and that he accepted a match as agent plenipotentiary of Immanity, then perhaps all memory of him could be erased from Immanity. And from myself—but even so..."

Steph reacted to Jibril's words with a gasp.

"*Memories of him wouldn't disappear from those who weren't his property or constituents*—so we could ask another race!"

"Precisely. I shall at once shift to the embassy of the Eastern Union to confirm this—also..."

Genuflecting before the door, lowering her head:

"...Afterward, I shall accept any punishment for my unsightly misconduct in proceeding on the presumption that my master*s* had been defeated—but please allow me a bit of time before this."

Jibril dissolving into void no sooner than she'd made this declaration. Vanished, leaving only a faint breeze filling the space left following the transmigration of matter. Steph, left alone, found herself at a loss for what to do but for the time being called through the door:

"Uh, er...Sh-Shiro...are you all right?"

...But by then, Shiro's mind was already elsewhere.

—The definite possibility that her brother existed. Having touched on a piece of it, her thoughts, which had been frozen, reactivated rapidly. A revelation of her hope in Sora—her brother—and the *evidence* that would turn that hope into certainty. Peeling her heavy body from the bed, standing up, she made her way to the center of the room as if crawling. Her wet ruby eyes, always half closed. She opened them wide and surveyed the room, sweeping her gaze so as not to miss a speck of dust, her thoughts accelerating faster.

(...If Brother, really...existed, then, why, did he...create, this situation?) Were she to accept Steph's hypothesis, then this situation had been *prepared by her brother.* All she could do was unravel why he might have done it—what her brother was thinking...but.

—Her brother's thoughts, which offered up play styles that sneered at conventional wisdom as easily as breathing. To divine the machinations of whom she felt she could never catch up to in an eternity?

...It was impossible. She hadn't a prayer. However, her brother had left her definite clues and decisive information.

"...There's, no way...Brother—would lose..."

—No, " " didn't lose. Which would mean—she had *agreed.* Her brother had believed in her, and she had believed in him. She had *known from the start* that a situation as maddening as this one would be the result. Why—hadn't she realized? Shiro tore at her hair.

(—I'm so...dumb! I'm so, stupid!) How could she look her brother in the eye now as the sister he was so proud of?

—Just because she had lost some memories.

"...How, could I...have, doubted—Brother?"

But now wasn't the time; she checked herself. This *game* her brother had entrusted to her—she had to end it.

Shiro forced her thought circuits to bend to her will—they could burn out for all she cared. Her little heart, responding to a scream from her brain that it needed more oxygen, beat out the fastest rhythm it could handle. Feeling her body heat rise precipitously, Shiro reviewed all of her memories. Pulling up every resource on Sora—every word, every move, like a silent movie. If the *present* in which she was floundering existed by her brother's design, he would have left her a hint. Her last memory of her brother: the words surfaced, the meaning of which she'd been unable to fathom.

—Shiro, we are always two in one.

"...Two, in one...Brother, would...never...leave me, alone..."

Why—why had she *woken up in what was supposed to be Steph's bedroom now*? Why hadn't she thought about it? Why hadn't she realized right away?! Shiro ground her teeth. This was exactly why she would never measure up to her brother. The answer was so simple—Sora, her brother—Brother—

(...*He is here*—he's always been here!) Shiro's eyes—glaring piercingly through the royal bedchamber—had no more tears.

Five moves remaining

...I am...Sora...Age... Now I forget.

...My darling sister—is Shiro, age eleven, a beauty with pretty white hair and red eyes. It's okay; I still remember.

"Shiro, are you there?"

The sense of a nod. My awareness and body, my memories... they're all a mishmash now. But I'm still just able to tell that the nod came from Shiro.

"—Shiro, you're still there, right?"

Again, the sense of a nod. All that supports me now. Even with most of my memories lost, still I know this much.

—That it's far beyond what I'd imagined. I've long lost my sight. I've got no feeling in my limbs. I hear voices—but I can't remember whose they are, where I am. I could never have imagined how terrifying it would be for everything to gradually fade away.

"Shiro...it's about time, I think...so you'll—"

The sense of a third nod with the feeling of desperate forbearance.

—I, know..., said a little voice. To these words, Sora says wryly, as if pleading:

"Will you do me a favor? My hand...well, it's got no more feeling...ha-ha."

With a laugh generously seasoned with despair, he continues.

"Anywhere. Just, hold me somewhere I can feel—so I don't go crazy."

His shoulder gripped tightly, Sora, slightly relieved, sighs. ***Ahh.*** **And places the piece in his mouth on the board.**

Shiro's heart rate as she glared into the void rose further.

—Organize all the information. Her brother's reminder: we're two in one. So she had also been a part of the game—no, it wasn't over—so she *was still* in the game. Her brother's conviction: We are always victorious before the game starts. So all of this was playing out as expected, exactly as intended. Her brother's assertion: We aren't the main character in a boys' manga. The main character in a boys' manga—*grows*. If this were a boys' manga, this would be Shiro's cue to grow as a person. She'd realize she could get along even without Sora, something like that—but her brother had *denied* that unequivocally. Her brother's faith: We are bound by a promise. The two of them…were two in one. Two comprised a finished product.

(…A, finished…product—doesn't, need…to grow!) Though her little head throbbed and started protesting in pain, Shiro ignored it and drove herself harder: Think more, think more—! Why was creating this situation *necessary*? Her brother had said: Let's go grab the last piece. He'd accepted a match in order to win a piece that would give them more of an edge over the Eastern Union in their game—

(…Then—who…is the enemy?) Her last memory with her brother. Her brother who had left behind cryptic words. At the time, he'd been looking from his throne at, talking to someone— But no matter how many times Shiro reviewed her memory—invisible. Why invisible? Why visible only to her brother? Someone using invisibility magic who—maybe Jibril would—in her memories—something—only—so—

(…Think more…think more, more, think more!!) Shiro's pulse, her thoughts—accelerated to a speed that by comparison stopped the hands of the clock on the wall.

—This would never be sufficient to retrace her brother's thoughts. Her brother's actions always had two or three—sometimes ten or twenty—meanings. He created strategies calculating backward from the results, using methods she couldn't even imagine. She wasn't capable of that creativity, that way of thinking beyond convention, that knack for shortcuts. (Then…I, just…have to, do this…my own, way!) Her body heat rising still more, the pain as if her head were being clamped in a vise making her sweat.

—It was an extremely inefficient, shall we say even *brutal*, way of thinking. The remaining memories, elements of the situation, clues, scenarios, information. Thousands, millions of possibilities. From each of these, she played out the billions, trillions of logical consequences.

—And *verified each one by brute force*. A method of deduction like a computer's, using the extremes of power. Shiro's little head which made it all possible broke into a cold sweat, throbbing as if it would split.

Finally—in roughly the time it took the clock's second hand to tick twice in what felt to Shiro like hours—in the back of her mind… someone—an answer emerged. All too fragmentary in her memory, that *someone*—whose face, looks, voice…even she couldn't remember. But hazily, an impression.

"…The one…we, played…to become monarch…"

The one who for the sake of Immanity—had even tried to use Elven Gard. What if someone like that *heard that her brother had bet the Immanity Piece*?

—Eastern Union, unbeatable piece, support of Elf—*spectators*.

"…Chla…mmy…!"

Just as she pronounced the name of *her brother's opponent* and felt everything come into place: As if an overrevved gear had flown off its axle—Shiro fainted.

■■■

Eight moves remaining

Let's run through this… I'm Sora. Shiro's brother, eighteen, virgin, socially incompetent, game vegetable. From another world——wait.

I played a game with a god, won, and came to this world with Shiro...and then?

—I see, it looks like my memories since I came to this world have been taken. But the real issue lies ahead...what is the *goal of this game?* If that's taken—it's all over.

...—

—It's okay. I can remember...*it's still mine.* Looks like its importance was just as I expected.

"...Just what are you after?"

A girlish voice asks keenly. My vision is gone. So I can't see her—but I've heard her voice. Her name is...Chlammy Zell. An informant for the country of Elves—Elven Gard. In this game, my *opponent.*

"Hmm, in what?"

Good, seems I can still talk, too.

"Don't play dumb. You're—playing to lose, aren't you?"

Without my sight, I was playing by the sound of the pieces on the board. But it seems I didn't go wrong... Everything is going fine.

"No? This is a move to win."

...Well, I think. Whatever underlay my conviction has become so slight. If you asked for proof, I couldn't give you a solid answer.

"—I see, so your *goal was for me to take your memory.*"

Yes—that was the kind of game it was. What you lose goes to your opponent. Since I no longer have my memories beyond coming to this world, that means Chlammy has them.

"...You're *no country's spy*—yes, that much I understand now."

I don't really know what this is about, but apparently she's understood me. The girl went on.

"—At this rate, you'll lose. Your existence will be taken, and even the fact that you existed will disappear. What intention do you have *beyond that*?"

...That I can't tell her. For that is my *true goal in this game.*

"Why do you ask? All you have to do is take it from me."

Yes—because that's the kind of game this is.

"...Very well. Then I shall fulfill your wish and take everything from you."

Chlammy makes a clack on the board. Using the sound to play back the move mentally—I quietly form a grin.

"——Wha...what is this?!"

With a shrill—no —almost shrieking voice, Chlammy stiffens.

—At the same time, *something* floods out of me and disappears.

"Wh-what...in the world...are you?!"

What she's asking me is exactly what she'd just screeched—— *who are you?*

—Okay, let's run it over one more time. I'm...Sora. Shiro's brother and.........and what?

"——?!"

An indescribable chill, a feeling that threatens to freeze and shatter my whole body, overwhelms me. Who am I? Where am I? Where did I come from? Where have I been?! *Unbecoming* myself—a fear that can't be described. Unable to take it, my teeth chatter, I shake, and I know this through senses that are but a husk of what has been taken away. Somewhere in my head, shouting: *You knew this! It's as planned. It's all right.*

—This fear as I gradually vanish is *as planned*? Bullshit! If I planned on this terror, who did I think I was?! Did I think I was capable of staying sane through this—?

"...Brother..."

But. The aching chill of absolute zero.

"...I'm, here...for you."

With these few words, the frost melted too readily to fathom and receded.

"—Yeah...you are, aren'cha?"

I'm...Sora. Proud brother of my darling sister Shiro. Now I'm—playing a game. *Losing for now, but ultimately to win.* That's all. As long as I know that, that's plenty. There's no problem at all. Whispering this in my heart, I clench my chattering teeth firmly to shut them up. To pick up the next piece—I slowly open my mouth.

■■■

—...

"Master?!"

"Shiro!! Are you all right?!"

At the sounds of Jibril and Steph's voices calling her worriedly, Shiro's consciousness rose back to the surface.

—Apparently she had collapsed. Finding herself in Steph's arms, assessing the situation—

"...!"

—finding her brother nowhere in her line of sight wherever she fixed her gaze, she almost leaped out of herself again. But somehow she managed to anchor herself with her thoughts.

—Her brother was *in this room*. Which meant—there was nothing more to fear.

"It's, o...kay..."

As Shiro, holding her throbbing head, tried to raise her sweat-drenched body, Steph held her back.

"It is not okay! Suddenly going silent and then collapsing like that—do you know how worried I was?!"

Noticing that Steph's eyes as she shouted were faintly red.

"...Sor-ry..."

Shiro mumbled quietly. Meanwhile, Jibril, who had been keeping an unnatural distance from Shiro, said as if having made up her mind—

"Master, I have something to tell you. I went to check about Sora—*Master...*"

As Jibril tried to give her confirmation report from the embassy of the Eastern Union—

"...Never, mind..."

Shiro interrupted her.

"...Brother...*exists*..."

"—Yes, just as you say. Please mete out any punishment—"

Poking at the embassy of the Eastern Union—at Ino Hatsuse—Jibril had been able to confirm definitively that "Sora" existed. For her, one who had doubted the assertions of her lord and lady, to have even entertained the notion of her lord and lady's defeat—

"...Okay...a, command."

"Yes, Master, speak the word."

Jibril, ready to comply without hesitation if her lady demanded her life then and there. But Shiro's reply was soft with only with a somewhat rushed edge.

"...Help, me...find...Brother..."

Jibril received these words as though they were divine revelation. And as if to say, *Now it's really okay*, Shiro gently let go of Steph's arm and stood on unsteady feet. The glint in her eyes once again normal, Shiro cast her gaze upon her servants and asked:

"—You, two...what, were you, doing...yesterday?"

As if she already knew their responses ahead of time, it was more of a confirmation than a question. Looking at each other, Steph and Jibril answered.

"Yesterday—I had my hands full with the protests, but in the corner of my eye, I saw you playing games on the throne."

"Yes, and I was with her."

—But Shiro authoritatively declared that this was wrong.

"...That was...the day, before yesterday...the *nineteenth*..."

While the two of them exchanged glances, Shiro pressed on.

"...Different question...where...were you...that, night?"

Having this put to them pointedly, Steph and Jibril searched their memories. But.

"——......"

They couldn't remember a thing. Noting Shiro's expression which seemed to imply that this was only natural, Jibril inquired—

"Master, do you mean that you remember last...no, the night before last?"

"...No, so...*that's, fine*."

—She was confirming the fact that the *memories that had been erased from all of them*. In other words—

"Then you mean—*the game ran from the night before last through yesterday*?"

Spurred by her oath to help, Jibril spun her brain at full speed to keep up, and Shiro nodded.

"Excuse me, but what do you mean?"

Steph looked puzzed, as if she didn't get it after all, prompting Jibril to explain.

"Lord Shiro had memories that we did not, and we had memories that Lord Shiro did not. *This caused confusion*—however, if there are memories that have disappeared from all of us, that changes things."

Steph looking all the more confused. Jibril distilled it further—

"It is proof that *all of us* are participating in the game and that the player is the only one with influence over all of Immanity—the agent plenipotentiary."

—Yes. And now all that remained—

"...Next...Steph...let's check."

"Y-yes, Your Majesty, please tell me your will."

Shiro staring at her with an expression more serious than Steph remembered ever having seen before. Bowled over by an eleven-year-old girl, Steph's reply had been quite solemn, her voice cracking as she prepared herself.

—It took her a few seconds to grasp the situation.

".........Ex-excuse me...what are you doing?"

If Steph wasn't misunderstanding or hallucinating, she was watching Shiro—still wearing that same severe mien—as her two little hands...those hands groping her—

"...I'm...squeezing...your, breasts..."

Shiro carried on unabated with gestures befitting such cute onomatopoeia as: *squish squish, boing boing.*

"—...Uhh, um, how am I supposed to react to this?"

Utterly unfazed by her question, Shiro merely nodded once, asking quizzically:

ぽにょ
PONYO (BOING)
...
...
MUNYO (SQUISH)
PONYO

"...Doesn't, it, *turn you on*?"

"Of—of course it doesn't! If it did, that would disqualify me as human in so many ways!"

As if having received the verification she required, Shiro let go.

"...Even though...I told, you...to fall, in love with me?"

"——Oh..."

...It was true. If Shiro had been the one with whom she'd been required by the Covenants to fall in love, Steph should have felt something. In other words, it meant that the one who'd demanded she fall in love with him was Sora... As Steph finally wrapped her brain around it, Jibril interjected apologetically.

"Master, may I ask...*it was not necessary* to confirm that, correct?"

"...Right..."

Shiro nodded dismissively without any apparent interest.

"—Pardon?"

"...Since, I, already, know...Brother's, here..."

"...Then may I ask for what purpose you fondled me?"

Steph, looked broken, as if to say, *After I worried about you so much, Shiro—!*

"...As thanks."

"How does that constitute thanks?! What do I gain from having my breasts—"

But what Shiro said next stopped her rant short.

"...Because...without you...I wouldn't, have realized—"

Then—just as Shiro was about to utter her next words—it occurred to her. Had she ever spoken them to anyone but her brother? She considered.

—*No* was her conclusion. Perhaps for this reason, Shiro awkwardly, ineptly, averted her gaze and blushed before articulating...

"...Thank, you...Steph..."

Her words and the sincerity of her expression left Steph breathless. Though for the next few days she would be clutching her head, Shiro wouldn't notice Steph's turmoil as to whether or not having her heart *skip a beat* for an eleven-year-old girl was something abnormal. Ignoring Steph's conundrum, Jibril asked quietly.

"With that, Master...may I assume that the situation is *fully grasped*?"

"...Mm."

Her brother figured that if he bet the Immanity Piece, Chlammy—Elven Gard—would come to him... Her brother, having *summoned* Chlammy thusly, must have been trying to win her to his side.

"...Just, one...more thing."

Only one question remained, but it was the crux. It was—the game itself. But even for this, almost all the answers had already coalesced in Shiro's thoughts.

—Her brother knew he would be challenged. And that his opponent would be Chlammy, and by extension Elf, Elven Gard. But considering their memories were being rewritten before the covenant was sealed, there had to be magic involved. A game prepared by Elf?—No. Taking on Rank Seven, Elf, her brother had to have anticipated the involvement of magic.

"...Brother, accepted...with a game, made...by, Jibril."

Without a doubt, he had answered with a game with the power to resist cheating by means of Elven magic. There was only one—among *them*—who could achieve that.

"—By me, you say?"

Yes, the Rank Six. Jibril the Flügel, capable of building an entire virtual world.

"...Jibril...could you, build it? *A game, that erases, memories...*"

Having been asked, Jibril thought deeply. If her master told her now to build such a game...?

"I could build a virtual world like that of Materialization Shiritori...but this is the real world..."

"...What about—with Elf, *together*?"

"T-together—?! With those *woodland rubes*?!"

Heartfelt dismay colored her voice. Such an idea had probably never even entered her imagination. But with Shiro's eyes fixed on her, Jibril gave the matter serious consideration and concluded:

"—It would depend on the skill of the Elf mage… But it might be possible. In terms of the absolute quantity of power available, we of Rank Six are superior. However, when it comes to weaving a complex rite…Rank Seven, Elf—is our better by a wide margin."

Jibril, from whom an admission lowering her own position was unheard-of. But now, having committed such an atrocity as to doubt her lord…being scrutinized by her master's gaze…what pretense could she uphold?

"For instance—if I provided the core of the Materialization Shiritori board, and an Elf mage wove the game around it…then it might be possible to weave a space-time distortion spell of this scale."

But there was still something missing. There was still a necessary component, surmised Shiro.

"…Also…they can't, build in…cheats. Can you, be sure?"

"Yes."

Shiro's concern was dismissed by Jibril forthright.

"To enact a rite inducing space-time distortion of this magnitude, a quantity of spirit far exceeding the limits of any Elf would be required. In the end, it would be I who would launch the game. Were there an impropriety in the rite, I would detect it thereupon."

"…Positive?"

"Yes, if this series of events has been brought about by magic, I have a feel for the amount of power that would be required."

Jibril, looking around, went on.

"Frankly speaking—it is on the level of the Heavenly Smite I unleashed upon the capital of Elf in the Great War."

Smoothly, she continued as if relating a trifle.

"I remember that, as I let loose a single blow with the intent of *wiping all trace of the city from the land*, the Elves attempted to block it with a spell that took the spirit-corridor-connected nerves of three thousand Elf mages and their lives to deploy, and still they were unable to stop it."

Shiro , deciding it pointless to be surprised at anything Jibril said by now, carried on with her musing. But Steph, unable to take it, let out a jab at the decisive weapon before her.

"Y-you…just what were you doing?!"

"Elf has developed their magical arts since the war, but the absolute quantity they can handle has not changed. If we assume that this space-time distortion is part of the game, under the direction of my masters, then the one who launched it is me. I could not possibly overlook an impropriety."

Jibril continued unfazed, her conviction absolute.

—In other words, the answer had *been in this room all along*. Somewhere in this living space littered with countless games was the *base*. The ongoing game's—*board*. But looking around, no such item presented itself. Then—

"…Jibril…in this room…there, should be…a magic, response…"

Her brother was in the room—but had been rendered imperceptible. This could mean that the *game board itself, also*, was excluded from Shiro's perception.

"…The day and a half we lost…our memories from the game… then, we can't…perceive, the game, either…"

But even if it was excluded from their perception, *if the game was ongoing*, then there had to be magic in use—

"…Let me investigate."

The Flügel could sense no magic there. But—unwilling to doubt her master again, Jibril spread her wings and opened her amber eyes.

"Eek—what…is this?"

Even Shiro and Steph, who weren't supposed to be able to detect any magic, were all but flattened by the pressure. Jibril had moved an obscene quantity of spirits—the source of the magic. Her halo spun wildly over her head, and there was an illusion as if the room itself was swaying—

"—I have located it."

This phrase was enough to make Shiro and Steph's faces spontaneously relax, but Jibril pointed to a corner of the room.

"…However, I must apologize. The best I can do is to sense that, over there, a field is deployed that *blocks perception*. If, as my master infers, this is an Elf rite using a game-board core provided by myself, then I suspect that overcoming this barrier to perception—is impossible."

"...!"

Biting her nails, Shiro groaned.

—One more step. The answer was lying right there before them, and yet—

"A-around here? I'll see if I can find anything."

Steph walked around the area Jibril indicated, lowering her eyes to the floor—but, suddenly, as if she had tripped on something, Steph fell spectacularly and did a face-plant.

"...Dora, I feel that falling when there is nothing to trip on is laying it on a bit thick for your character."

But Steph's gaze as she got up and turned back was blank.

"...What? I *fell*? *I* fell?"

At these words, Shiro and Jibril realized at the same time.

"...!"

"Even if it is not perceptible, *it is there*. It simply eludes awareness even on touch, I suppose?"

Nodding at Jibril's words, Shiro walked forward. Even if you couldn't perceive it, it was there—you could touch it. Completely invisible, imperceptible even to the sense of touch, a game board was there. Then Shiro noticed something near where Steph fell. A little box of pieces—white on one side, black on the other—engraved with *Chinese numerals*. And another box with similar pieces, engraved with *Elf numerals*. Surmising the true nature of these pieces was very simple.

"...Othello...pieces."

"Whatever might this mean? Are these the pieces for the game?"

To Jibril, wondering why they would be able to see the pieces but not the board, Shiro responded.

"...Be-cause...they, *haven't been used*."

The pieces that hadn't been used, which they could still perceive. A game that took away their memories and their very perception of the game—*a game that was not yet over.* Shiro connected it all in her mind by a single thread. The rules were probably—

"A game, where you split…your, *memories*…and *existence*… among the pieces…and take them, from each other."

Jibril was first to react to Shiro's whisper followed after a beat by Steph.

"M-Master, if I may be so bold…"

"Wh-what kind of lunatic would play that?!"

Yes—if Shiro's conjecture was correct, it was, with no room for doubt, a game of *madness.* But if the rules were as surmised, then, after all—

"…Brother, you're…so, amazing…"

Shiro felt a trickle of cold sweat at the realization that at last—she had arrived at her brother's intent.

Before the first move

"—Come, then, let's review the game's rules."

Sora speaks to Chlammy, sitting in the chair across the table from him. And behind him, Shiro, Steph, and Jibril. And, behind Chlammy, the Elf girl.

"We shall split the concepts that constitute us into thirty-two pieces each—and play Othello."

Playing in his hand with a piece with white on one side, black on the other, with a numeral engraved, Sora continues.

"The pieces have numbers engraved, lower numbers for more important concepts. Like your memories, personality, body, and stuff, I guess? Otherwise it's just normal Othello. You flip over the opponent's pieces—*and take the opponent's existence.*"

The game Sora had thought of, Jibril had provided the power

source for, and the Elf girl had woven. Though Sora explained the rules casually, they were by no means ordinary, and everyone swallowed audibly from the tension.

"Also note that importance is judged by the game's magic according to *their importance in your unconscious*. Which would mean that you can't tell yourself what pieces govern what."

Sora seemed quite happy, but—

"...You don't know what you're gonna lose given which pieces are taken—is that a rush or what?"

To Sora, stirring up madness in his eyes—Chlammy responds with eyes calm and cold.

"I want to expose your true identity and backers. You want to expose as much as possible of Elven Gard's hand. It does seem a game in which our interests would be aligned."

"Correct. And then, the winner gets back everything that was theirs—*and the loser gets back nothing*."

At the meaning of these words, a chill jolts down Steph's spine.

"—If you lose your *personality* and then lose the game—ha-ha, now that'll be something, won't it?

"Oh, and one more thing. Unlike normal Othello, *you don't get to pass*. Even if there's no place you can play your piece to capture, you still have to play it. I'm sure you can imagine the endgame in such a situation, in which you have to place the pieces with low numbers...right?"

But Chlammy, seemingly unintimidated, keenly points out a hole in the rules.

"Then—what happens when you physically can't continue?"

They'd lose their senses, their very bodies, their memories of the game, etc.

"For each of us... In my case, Shiro or one of the other two will play for me. For you, it'll be that sweet little Elf girl. Therefore, *everyone here is a participant*—all of us together are going to start a game under *Aschente*."

But that still leaves a question unresolved—namely.

"But, in the course of taking *everything* **from the opponent, it is quite conceivable that all memories of oneself might be taken from one's allies, so that's when you really can't continue. The game's over. Whoever has the most pieces wins.**

"We'll need an objective judge of victory, so we'll have the *game board itself* **do it. Yeah?"**

"Why, that's quite so. I have, after all, woven the rite thus already."

"I, too, have confirmed this. Please be at ease, Master."

The Elf girl who is Chlammy's partner and Jibril each nod. Jibril's eyes deny the most threatening possibility—that there could be a trick. Mm, Sora nods and continues.

"—But for everything to go back the way it was after the game is over...would be boring, wouldn't it?"

Yes, this is magic. But even with the massive power supplied by Jibril, it is not possible to make the results permanent. Reading Chlammy's inner wish to *wipe out Sora's very existence,* **Sora smirks.**

"To make results *persist* **after the game—there are two things we're gonna bet."**

Raising one finger, Sora went, first.

"One is *permanent setting of the game results*—**i.e., of the erasure, trading, and retention of the traces of each other's existence we've transferred back and forth. And, apart from that, we'll get one other demand."**

Anticipating his intent, Chlammy continues.

"...And that is your real demand, I take it?"

"*Indubitably.* **Without that, even if you managed to wipe out my existence,** *you couldn't do anything about Shiro.***"**

That is, after all, Chlammy's goal as she aims to usurp the role of agent plenipotentiary of Immanity, he hints.

"Likewise, I would be unable to get your Elf. It follows that our second demand—"

"—is to take each other's partner, I see."

In other words, if Chlammy wins, she'll get Shiro with her memories of Sora lost—the agent plenipotentiary of Immanity. And, if Sora wins, he'll get the greatest mage of Elven Gard.

"But, you know, we'll still say you can change your demand after you win."

At this, Chlammy smiled superciliously.

"...Do you think I will take pity on you and allow you to exist?"

"Ha-ha, that's a good one; of course not."

Sora, smiling right back and dismissing the notion, peers into Chlammy's eyes.

"If I'm gone, even if you bind Shiro by the Covenants, she'll probably be of *no use*. And I can assume the same about yours. So *retention* might not do it—we might need a covenant of *suicide* or *personality change*—ya know?"

A tremor goes down the spines of everyone present except Shiro and Sora.

"So, to sum things up—we're gonna take from each other, betting *each other's existence* and *the right to kill our partners*."

Yes—it's a game of all or nothing, including even their partners. It's insane—is Steph the only one thinking this? Shiro, who made part of the bet, perhaps isn't even considering the scenario of her brother's defeat. Or perhaps has been fully briefed on his strategy and understands it—in any case, her eyes are half open as usual.

"Till the final move that renders one unable to continue, till one's existence is taken in its entirety—by these rules, come now—has everyone steeled themselves to begin the game?"

Upon Sora, clowning and looking around at everyone, their gazes collect. Sora, who thought up and laid out this game of dubious sanity. Before this man, somehow maintaining composure, Chlammy thinks. Yes, this—*is a game Sora thought up*. The rules look fair at a glance—and that's just why Chlammy has to suspect them. For, in a game in which he was challenged, he had to set things up so as to be favorable to him. Somewhere there's a

loophole, or else— Chlammy shifts her gaze to the girl who is his partner. But the girl just shakes her head to the side.

—Can't read anything. Can't grasp the meaning. But she said there was no trick in the game. The Elf girl who wove the game rite herself said she could not build a trick into the game. But conversely that it was inconceivable Jibril could have built in a trick.

"—...Very well."

Then her only choice is to expose his true intent *within the game*. Whatever Sora's intent is, it is of no consequence, for on her side is the power of Elf, she decides. Shiro, Steph, Jibril, and Sora. And Chlammy, and the Elf girl, lightly raise their hands up—and speak.

"—*Aschente*!"

Shiro held a piece white on one side, black on the other, 参 [III] engraved on each. Staring at empty space—no, at a board *that was there but just could not be seen*. This must be a game of Othello in which one's existence, memories, were split into thirty-two pieces, and you *took them from each other*. The pieces they were left with all had small numbers—which probably meant they were important. That they were pieces that might end the game in the same move if they were taken, and therefore had been left. But the one who had laid out these rules—was the party challenged, that is, *her brother*. Which meant that there was a meaning in playing this game, and even in disappearing. Then it must be— Shiro closed her eyes and thought.

—It was puzzling why her brother had left her alone. However, once the answer came into view, it was clear as day. The first reason was very simple. His intent to *give her his memories intentionally* while temporarily getting his ass kicked.

(...I, could...never do, that.) Imagining it, Shiro laughed sadly to herself and came to this conclusion. If she had tried to do what her brother had done...she could not imagine staying sane. Just finding him no longer by her side had been enough to make her for a time doubt her brother's very existence.

—To be forgotten would be one thing.

—But to forget him—she was confident she'd never stay sane. Shiro stared at the invisible board, the board she couldn't even perceive by touch. Indeed, she could not see the board. However— Her brother hated sunlight. He wouldn't sit by the window. Her brother when they slept—even when they sat together—picked the side that put Shiro by the wall. Her brother understood that open places felt lonely and always blocked her from the open space. She couldn't see the board. But all her memories of her brother, his quirks, his mannerisms, his kindness. Exposed the location of the chair in which he sat, even the spot he gave to her, as if she could see it.

(...Brother...is...here...) In void, yet for sure, she sensed where her brother was. Feeling the corners of her eyes getting hot, still Shiro held it back and went on thinking.

(...And, this...is the second...and...the, biggest...reason!) Shiro took the piece labeled 参 [III], turned its white side up, and sandwiched it between her fingers. There was no room for doubt. Whether her brother was white or black. If he'd left the final moves to *Shiro*—that answered it. The match she still couldn't see, couldn't even perceive. The board state she didn't remember even in its early stages. Much less know midgame. The moves her brother had made to lose intentionally, and then to let Shiro win. The moves that had brought the opponent right into his trap, that her brother *had led the opponent to make*. And all the positions her brother had taken for her so that she could turn the tables.

She read them all—and would turn the tables in just three moves.

This...only Shiro could do! With conviction, Shiro lowered her hand—*click*, an inaudible sound hit the earlobes of the three.

* * *

The next moment.

"Uh—gh—!"

"Ow—...wh-what is this!"

Shiro, and Jibril and Steph, held their heads at the ache that attacked. As if in response to the move Shiro had laid down, noise ran through their heads. The Othello board they'd not been able to perceive appeared, and, flip, flip, the black board turned white. And—their lost memories of a day and a half—surged back—

■■■

——*The nineteenth: Daytime......*

It was, unmistakably, the throne room where she had been playing with her brother.

"Oh, you're finally here. You ever heard of timeliness?"

Where her brother was looking, there were two girls. The black-haired girl with the black veil, Chlammy. And, apparently not even trying to hide the two long Elfin ears peeking through her hair, an Elf girl.

"...You speak as if you knew we would come, do you—then, of course..."

To Chlammy, Sora replied with a smile.

"Yeah, I know why you're here. I'm ready anytime, of course."

"Then hurry. It is imperative that you disappear before the Immanity Piece is surrendered."

"Shiro, listen closely."

"...Mnn?"

"I believe in you."

——*The nineteenth: Evening......*

"—So that's the idea, but, Jibril, can you make it?"

To these game specifications that could hardly be the product of a sound mind, still Jibril confessed.

"—I sincerely apologize, but it is beyond my abilities. Such drastic game remodeling—"

"I didn't say you have to do it by yourself. You and that Elf Chlammy brought make it together, okay?"

To the Elf girl who would never volunteer her name, Sora turned.

"…Create a spell with a Flügel, together? Sir, I'm afraid I must decline. ♥"

"What a rare coincidence. I, too, could hardly be pressed to accept. ♥"

To the two, sparks flying between their eyes, Sora disinterestedly insisted.

"Oh, yeah, then I'm not playing. You guys pack up and go home, okay?"

As Sora tersely dismissed them, still Chlammy said to the Elf girl.

"…I thought you said you were going to help me."

"Well, of *course*, but to work with that devil…nghh… All right, fiine."

"…Brother."

Having heard the rules Sora specified, Shiro looked up at Sora worriedly.

"Shiro, we are always two in one."

——*The nineteenth: Night*……

With the "core" of Jibril's Materialization Shiritori board in her hand, the Elf girl muttered:

"Why, to use spirits in such an explosive manner that could destroy one's very spirit corridors, it's simply *madness*."

"My apologies. It appears that, in merely scooping from the stream which feeds spirit circuits, I have created the false impression of a bomb to those who merely have long ears. In the future, I shall think to attach a note that explains, 'NOT FOR DIMWITS.'"

"You guys… Seriously, is there anyone you can get along with?"

"But, like, there was this one Flügel, during the War, and when I think of just how many of us were sacrificed with that one strike…

Always acting so superior, and then it's a Heavenly Smite, why, it's just so childish."

"If you'd only known your place and refrained from casting an antiflight spell in the sky, I would not have so much as taken notice of you, so I must say, you got what you deserved. You made me fall and get a bump on my head. Who can blame me for getting carried away and slaughtering you all?"

"Look, whatever, just shut up and build it, both of you! The date's gonna change!!"

——*The twentieth: Day*……

"…Now, the date has changed, if you'll observe."

Sora, squinting coolly at Jibril. And Chlammy, likewise squinting, looked at their partners.

"I-I deeply apologize. This pointy-ear kept bringing the circuit to the brink of runaway, you see."

"A-and every time you tried to stop runaway by force, I had to recompile the rite from scratch, you knoww?"

With a deep sigh, Sora, cheek in hand, muttered.

"Okay, whatever, ahem— So, shall we go over the rules one more time?"

"…Brother."

"Shiro, your brother's grateful that you worry about him, but relax. You know, don't you?

"Shiro, we are bound by a promise.

"Shiro, we are always victorious before the game starts.

"—Let's go grab the last piece we need to swallow up the Eastern Union."

"…Mm!"

Shiro nodding firmly, Sora stroked her head and said.

"Come, let the game begin!"

——*The twentieth: Night*……

"……"

Shiro's right hand gripping Sora's shoulder tightly. Her left hand, gripping with even more force, too much, dug in her nails and drew blood. Before her eyes, her brother's memory, arms, legs, senses being taken, all she could do was watch.

—That was to believe her brother. To repay her brother's words when he said that he would believe in her. For now, she could only bear it. Her countenance was such as to even make Steph hesitate as to whether to stop the game, but, perhaps unable to watch any longer, she covered her face with her hands and groaned as if about to cry. And Jibril, likewise, no longer could say anything in the face of the resolve of her two lords. Only watch their every movement with both eyes wide.

"—Come now, it's about over."

Chlammy said this with a piece in her hand. She herself could hardly be called intact. Everyone there had lost some memories, and she had had enough shaved away that she could tell. But the board was clearly dominated by black—by Chlammy, overwhelmingly.

"...You do have quite the interesting set of memories. But still, as ever, I cannot grasp your intent."

Though she must have already taken almost all of Sora's memories. *She still couldn't grasp his true aim.* Wincing at Sora's memories—at the flashbacks, Chlammy said.

"You have only three pieces remaining. That your memories of your true aim would stand among the principal concepts constituting you, I must tip my hat...but just what do you mean to do—with this."

Snap, Chlammy played her piece.

"I think that's it."

As if in response to her words, Sora vanished before their eyes. And the three who, until just now, had been watching the match with emotions unguarded. Now, like dolls, with eyes devoid of sentience or light. Ambled, as if they couldn't see Chlammy, or even the game, out of the room. They, the participants, must have lost memories that included the fact that the game had even taken place. And Shiro alone went straight to bed and began the quiet breath of sleep.

"...Now no one will play for him. Sora is gone. Cannot continue— I suppose I win."

To the end, she had been unable to read Sora's true intent. He'd dumped on her any number of sickening memories, but what—

"Chlammy...something's funny."

The game board was supposed to declare victory.

—But there was no sign of the end of the game.

"What is this? I thought you said there was no trick!"

"Th-there isn't, I'm sure! Why, I was the one who wove the riite?"

"Then how you explain this—do you mean to say they *can* still continue?!"

Flashing before Chlammy's eyes, Sora's three remaining pieces. The most important pieces constituting him, labeled 壱 (I), 弐 (II), and 参 (III).

"—Wait. If his existence has already vanished, then what in the world are these three pieces?"

Could it be—could it be that even his own existence. Was not as important to him as his *strategy for winning the game*? That was absurd—but, if true, it would explain why she had been unable to take that memory—

"Chlammy, what will you do?"

"What can I do?!"

If anyone was capable of force-quitting this game, it could only be that Flügel.

"What is there to do but sit here with our memories hacked up— and wait!"

As if raging at the game board that apparently still hadn't judged them unable to continue, Chlammy bemoaned:

"...What is this? what did he do, that man—?!"

The man who'd just lost unceremoniously and disappeared. Yet his memories having been taken almost entirely by Chlammy, in the void, she saw. Him *smirking in victory*, in her imagination—and was unable to keep her legs from shaking.

* * *

——......Yes, Sora had indeed incorporated a "trick." Just as Chlammy had suspected, this game was made from the start to favor Sora. But—its methodology...could not be fathomed by anyone. Even the one who had made the game, using Elf magic—could not reveal it. For this trick *was a cheat that worked without any cheating.*

—For, in this game, the importance of the pieces was determined as a reflection of the unconscious. And, under normal circumstances, *the most significant concepts constituting oneself* were known to no one.

—Yes.

■■■

"*...Except, Brother...and, me.*"

Shiro grinned faintly and stared at the board that had shown itself. So *this was it*—the true form of the trick her brother had planted.

"I remember now. Even allowing that the game's rules dictated it, to forget my *master*..."

Even allowing that it was inevitable by the design of the game to which she had consented. Jibril hung her head at her worthlessness in doubting her lord and attempting to wipe away his existence.

"B-but why did Sora disappear; it was intentional, was it not?!"

Steph, likewise having gotten back most of her lost memories, raised her voice. But even so, even Shiro had no memory that would suggest Sora's true purpose.

—No, probably she'd *never* had any such memory to begin with. Her brother must not have told her his true purpose, Shiro thought. Because if that memory was taken, the whole plot would be ruined. But it didn't matter—because now Shiro *knew.*

—Othello was a finite, zero-sum, two-player game with perfect information. Its patterns were simpler than those of shogi or chess, and perfect play had been clearly established. *To win by normal methods*, all Sora had to do was let Shiro play for him. Probably, why he hadn't done that but made it Othello—was to make it *easy for Shiro to read.*

...Then, from the void, something independently placed a black piece. Hesitantly, waveringly... Yes—as Sora had specified, in this game, *you couldn't pass.* The substitute—Shiro—had played a single move. That *blocked off Chlammy completely*, a move without a crack that Sora had prepared. This meant she'd have to place an important piece in vain—it was only natural that she'd hesitate.

...Awestruck by her brother's strategy, she took in hand the piece labeled 弐 (II). Shiro knew by now. The concept governed by the piece in her hand, showing 弐, and her brother's true purpose.

—Therefore, feeling so much as sympathy for her opponent, she said.

"...No, one could...read something...like, this...Brother...you're amazing."

Shiro thus smiled and played her second move. The pieces that flipped over this time washed almost the entirety of the board white. Indistinctly, Chlammy and the Elf girl—and. The visage of the brother started to reappear to Jibril and Steph, who widened their eyes. All the while, Shiro fought back what was threatening to pour out of her own eyes. The game set up by her brother, who had disappeared from her phone, and from the memories of Immanity, and of Jibril. From this game could be read—the meanings of the three pieces that remained. They were—

参 [III]—How to win the game

弐 [II]—His absolute trust in Shiro

And 壱 [I]—

"...All, of me, of Shiro... myself..."

These were the identities of the elements that constituted Sora as a person, *more essentially than his very self.* How could she be so sure? The answer was simple. Because, if their roles were reversed—Shiro was sure that hers would be the same. Without her brother, she wouldn't be Shiro. That the things at risk—her brother himself, the possibility of defeat—would be more important than herself—was *self-evident.* Sora, understanding that, had known from the start that he would disappear and then Shiro would step in to turn the tables—with a trick like this, even if you saw through it, what could you possibly do? On the board turning white, shakily, uneasily…a black piece was placed.

"…Come on, Brother…"

And, as if it had been what she'd been waiting for.

"…Come, back—!"

Before Shiro's eyes, once she slammed down the piece labeled 壱 on the board, Sora clearly reappeared.

—With a victory margin of just four pieces, the board emanated a voice that declared, "Winner: Sora." The winner announced, Shiro leaped at the same time. The first thing Sora said was:

"Okay, Shiro, you can hit me now. I'm read—"

But Shiro, unhesitatingly burying her face in Sora's chest, was just faster. Face hidden in her brother's chest, leaking big tears, she only said:

"…I'm, sorry…I'm sor-ry…I should have—realized…!"

Jibril and Steph, unable to follow the situation, could only stare. But a voice came from an unexpected direction.

"Chlammy! Please, Chlammy! Can't you hear mee?!"

Turning their eyes toward the voice, what they saw. The Elf girl calling Chlammy, over and over, her countenance desperate, and…

Steph involuntarily covered her mouth and gasped. At the shell—no, to all normal eyes the *corpse* of Chlammy, limp in the chair.

…Steph still did not know how Sora had won. But, at the end Sora would have met had he lost in this game he proposed. With just one wrong move…she visualized Sora's fate, and her legs shook. Whatever she had lost—or perhaps having lost everything but her body.

Now the entity, the personality known as Chlammy—was gone. (Wh-what kind of person could play this game *with the intention of heavy sacrifice*?!)

—Filled inside with dread at this *game* that broke so far beyond her understanding, Steph looked at Sora. The game whose atrocious results she couldn't even have imagined before seeing them. At *its results*, Shiro still cried on as, drawing her close, Sora opened his mouth drily.

"—So, looks like *we* win. Time for my first demand, yeah?"

At his words, the Elf girl begged as if screaming.

"Wai—I'll do anything! Don't let Chlammy—please, anything but that!!"

But Sora looked back with eyes that had lost all temperature.

"...If I had lost and Shiro had made the same request, would you guys have accepted?"

Yes—this was a game under mutual consent by *Aschente*. Just as Sora said, in the same position, she could hardly have given a second glance...but—

"I-I know I have no right to ask such a thing! B-but you were the one who specified that the demands be changeable! Y-you can do anything you want with me—just don't...don't leave Chlammy—!"

Sora replied with the sadistic smile of a devil, as if swinging down the executioner's ax:

"Nnnope! I'll have you fulfill my demands *just as planned*. So, here we go—"

"No———nooooooooooooooooooooo!!!"

"Demand One: All memories we have taken from each other shall persist—*and all we have taken shall be returned*."

"—Huh...?"

At this statement, everyone made the same sound together.

"—Guh!—*Hh...hh...*"

At the same time, Chlammy came to as if she'd just remembered to breathe. But as Chlammy went on staring into space even after waking up, the girl ran to her.

"Chlammy! Chlammy, are you all right?! Do you know who you are?!"

At the girl's desperate voice, still Chlammy remained blank, her eyes vacant. Then, shaken bodily many times, she eventually showed signs of awareness returning.

"Yes...Right, I am all right... Rather..."

—Chlammy held her shaking shoulders and looked at Sora like a nightmare.

"I was merely dazed, unable to comprehend why that man—Sora—is all right."

—In an instant, at the execution of the covenant, the game board created by Jibril and the Elf made a boom. At this, the one who exuded the most cold sweat was, unexpectedly—Sora.

"O-oh, snap... Even with Jibril's core, I guess this request was pushing it..."

—A covenant that was theoretically impossible could not be carried out. It seemed that executing Sora's demand strained the capacity of the game board's magical power. Seeing Sora thus, Jibril came forth quietly.

"...Master. Next time, please allow me, as your servant, the indulgence of stopping you from engaging in such a game."

"*Denied.* When you think about the dudes we're gonna have to face in the future, we should be *happy* to only go through this crazy shit."

Still—went Sora. Stroking Shiro's head as she buried her face in his chest and cried, he said.

"Yeah, all right, I'll be a little more thoughtful how I do things. Honestly—it went beyond what I imagined."

"—It went beyond what you imagined? That's my line."

Chlammy, having had Sora's memories set fast in her, still could hardly believe them. Mere humans had really overcome a god and taken down a Flügel—but worse than *any of that was what had come before.* Touching upon Sora and Shiro's past, she had to say it. The many memories she had taken from Sora, set fast in her by the covenant. Twisting her face in fear with every flashback, Chlammy screamed.

"How—after experiencing all this, were you able to *keep your head on straight*?"

What elicited this shriek from Chlammy? If even Sora's psyche during the game had been taken at the end, she must have seen it. It could be that, or also—it could be *something even Shiro didn't know*. But the only one who would have an idea about it all, Sora, asked everyone as if surprised.

"Huh? Do I look like I have my head on straight?"

—No. Everyone there shook their heads.

A relationship of mutual trust going beyond normal bounds?—No. To put another person at the top of the list of elements that constitute oneself is not what is called *trust*. At that point, it was a *condition for existence*. These two, all metaphor and hyperbole aside, were truly—*two in one*. Warped. Broken. But, when you put them together, they joined as if so designed into a complete *one*. It defied comprehension. But, having touched upon Sora's past, Chlammy knew. Now she knew. *Fate*—these memories were too heavy for such a facile word, and yet none other arose. For these two—if they hadn't met—

"...Now, Demand Number Two."

Indeed, of the demands afforded by the covenant—there was still one remaining. The Elf girl braced herself, but Chlammy, having learned Sora's intent, checked her. "It's all right."

"Elf over there—'Fiel.' I receive *the right to alter one* of your memories. These days when you talk not with your fists but with *games*, you get it, right, Chlammy?"

Chlammy sighed and nodded.

"...Yes, I know what you mean—you want us to be *double agents*, correct?"

Sora smiled at the surprise of all around him. Chlammy spoke, chagrined.

"You've assumed that if you handed your memories to me, you could get me on your side without using the Covenants; how naive of you."

But her face was like that of a child who'd been inspired by a fascinating puzzle, and she smiled.

"—Fine. I'll play along; it is quite interesting—this *plan* of yours."

Seeing her, Fiel's understanding caught up. Sora's intent—*to share all his memories, to peek into Chlammy's memories*, and to set these fast. Without any binding force from the Covenants, to leave himself just one—*to alter her memory when the time came…* Considering the match with the Eastern Union—and, further on, everything else that would come into play— Having reached the conclusion, the Elf girl could only say this:

"I see… Well, I'll be honest—why, you've defeated us utterly."

Jibril and Steph could only stare blankly as ever. Shiro alone arrived at the meaning of these words, and she opened her eyes wide and mumbled.

"…Brother…you're amazing…"

"I know, right? You can praise your cool brother some more, you know."

With her face still buried snugly in Sora's chest, increasing the force in her hugging hands, Shiro replied to Sora's teasing.

"…Mm… My, cool…brother…"

"Mmnph— When you say it without sarcasm, it makes your brother embarrassed…whooph."

The moment's tension dispelled, Sora slumped to the floor, overcome by his fierce fatigue, Shiro still clinging to him. Stopping Steph and Jibril with his hand as they rushed forward in concern, Sora spoke.

"—Shiro…I can say it now, right?"

"…Mm, standing, by…ready, when you are."

And Chlammy also, holding the hand of the Elf girl—Fiel.
"Sorry, Fi...but do you mind if I also...?"
"Um, oh, why, certainly, please say what you like!"
Sora, Shiro, and Chlammy all drew in a deep breath together.

"Auughh, that was sooo scaryyy, I'm never gonna pull this shit agaiiiiin! Sorry, Shirooo!"
"Mm-mmghhh...H-hic...Hmghh..."
"Waaaaaaaaaaaaaaaaaaaaaah! I can't belieeeve this man! What's wrooong with him?!"

Ignoring their flabbergasted companions, the three poured out all their inner feelings like children, and they kept crying and crying until they fell asleep from exhaustion—

CHAPTER 2 BLUE ROSE

ORIENTATION

The next day—in a little conference room at the edge of the Elkia Royal Castle. There were Sora and Shiro, Steph and Jibril, and Chlammy and Fiel the Elf. Sora with an ironic grin, Shiro with half-open eyes as usual, and Chlammy, her gaze serene. These three, the previous day having bawled their heads off and then collapsed like logs, now showing no sign of this. If you looked closely, they all had slightly red eyes, but they had gotten their groove back.

"...So, why are we all here?"

The question everyone seemed to be waiting for someone to ask was taken up by Steph. As if he'd also been waiting, Sora answered.

"I have a certain understanding with Chlammy now through memory, but we're gonna *fight together*. We need to introduce ourselves, don't we?"

—*Fighting together*: what Chlammy had mentioned the previous day—being *double agents against Elven Gard*. At an exchange that hinted at something *even beyond that*, Jibril and Steph watched

Chlammy and Fiel. Chlammy—with her dark eyes and black hair, peering with a sharp gaze full of intellect, said straight:

"—I'm Chlammy Zell. Nice to meet you."

……As it seemed that was it. Sora had to go on.

"Uhh, same age as me, eighteen, height 158 centimeters, bust—"

"H-hey, you?! That's cowardly!"

Flusteredly stopping Sora as he slowly divulged her personal information, Chlammy shrieked.

"And she wears padded bras, but really—"

"F-fine, then! Fine, stop, I'll do it, all riiight!"

It was apparent to everyone but Chlammy that she had subtly broken into weeping, but anyway.

"B-but before that—Fi needs to be introduced before I can explain anything…"

Chlammy glancing over, the Elf girl called Fi opened her mouth.

"Hellooo, I am Fiel Nirvalen!"

From blond hair gently curled so as to look soft to the touch, the distinctive long ears of Elf pointing out—the girl who looked as if she were in her midteens introduced herself in a disarming voice.

"But everyone except that devil over there can just call me Fiii!"

This might have been what it meant for a smile to be like the sun. At Fi with her soft and gentle aura, yet having been called a devil, Jibril cocked her head as if to say, *Oh really*, and said.

"Well, then, you certainly have taken a dislike to me. I wonder why? It puzzles me."

—Was that supposed to be a joke, perhaps? As everyone looked coolly at Jibril, Sora, cheek in hand, muttered.

"Those are some words from someone who says she unleashed a 'Heavenly Smite' or some shit on their capital."

But, as if Sora's point had taken her entirely by surprise…

"What? As I have explained to you previously, clearly I had no culpability in—"

"Yes, you did! *A bump on the head versus the obliteration of a city?* Seriously, how do you even compare?!"

To Sora's commonsense observation, Fi piled on with a merry smile.

"If I may also add, at that time she made off with the whole stockpile of our grimoires. Why, it took us over eight hundred yeaars to reestablish the schemes of magic that were lost then, you know!"

Sora, drumming his fingers like hammers on the desk, spoke.

"—Ms. Jibril, your defense."

"Defense? Well, I never... Sir, Elf heads are only Rarity 2, and when you consider I used up all my power in that Heavenly Smite, don't you think that was a bit much? Even for me, it took about five years to recover?"

Who knew what a "Heavenly Smite" actually was, but anyway, it was apparently some attack that could *annihilate* an entire city. Finding that to draw on this much power had a price even for Flügel, the humans sighed with relief inside.

...Whether or not five years was an appropriate price.

"Thus, I availed myself of the books I observed, so that I would at least gain something from the battle. Now, in the age of the Ten Covenants—eh-heh-heh, when I look back, it was a good catch, geh-heh, eh-heh-heh-hehh!"

"The defendant, Jibril, is found—guilty."

"Why?!"

As Jibril pulled a face that suggested an immediate appeal, Sora ignored her. Worrying how in the world he could convince one whose brethren had been massacred to forgive the perpetrator.

"Uhh, well, I can call you Fi?"

"Why, of course!"

"If we're going to fight together, I want to get rid of grudges. How can I get you to forgive Jibril?"

As Sora got right to the point, Fi put her finger to her cheek, thinking in her spacy voice.

"Hmmm, why, that's hard to say."

But Chlammy spoke also, with her eyes closed and arms folded.

"Fi, we need her power for *Sora's plan*. I ask you as well."

Nghh... Sighing reluctantly, Fi made a proposal.

"All riiight, why, if you only lick my feet and say, 'Please forgive me, Fiel, Your Ladyship,' then I'll forgive youu. ♥"

"Oh, dear, dear, the conceit of this forest mongrel with her pretentious long ears has just crossed the heavens!"

As the two beamed at each other with black smiles. Yet, disinterestedly messing with a mobile game on Sora's lap, Shiro mumbled.

"...Jib-ril...guilty... *Punishment.*"

"Whaaaat, s-surely you don't intend to actually tell me to lick the feet of this ani—"

"...Punishment."

"Ngh, nghhhh...I do not grasp your reasoning, Master, but if you command..."

And Jibril crawled to Fiel's feet.

Lick, lick...

"—*(flatly) Ohh, please forgive me, Fiel, Your Ladyship.*"

"Whyy, then, I forgive youu!"

Just like that, Fi put her hands together and smiled as if she'd really forgiven the Flügel.

—Was that it? Sora wondered if this chick actually didn't even care about the past and had just wanted to pick on Jibril, but putting that aside for now.

"Ma-Ma-Ma—Master, d-do you have a moment?!"

Interrupting his thoughts, Jibril ran to him with her eyes gleaming over a major discovery.

"I-it is the depth of disgrace to have to lick the feet of such a base animal and apologize to her, but, how could it be?! I feel—when I think that it is a command at the behest of my masters, somehow...I get these shivers! Do you have any notion as to the true nature of this great—"

"All right, now, Chlammy, let's get on with the intro—"

As Sora tried to advance the conversation regardless of her, yet again...

"Excuse me, if we speak of grudges, I have my own."

"—Wha, Steph? The hell are you talking about?"

Thrusting a finger toward the cool-faced Chlammy, Steph howled:

"I'm talking about—h-her! Isn't this the one who cheated with magic to defeat me?!"

"It's your fault for falling for it. Okay, Chlammy, go on."

"Hey—?!"

Putting aside the curtly dismissed Steph, Chlammy spoke.

"Fi…is my childhood friend. To be precise—my *master*, actually."

To Shiro, momentarily failing to see her meaning, Jibril explained.

"Elven Gard is a democracy, but they promote the binding of races ranked lower than themselves by the Covenants—to put it bluntly, in a slave system."

"Wha… Then Chlammy is…"

To Steph, blurting this out, Chlammy nodded.

"Yes, since the time of my great-grandfather, we have been the *slaves* of the Nirvalen family. I was born and raised in Elven Gard."

With a wry smile at Steph, at a loss for words, Chlammy continued.

"It's no great matter… Everyone has a hardship or two to endure."

Seeing her glance toward Sora, Steph, and Jibril, and even Fi wondered what in Sora's past could possibly have made Chlammy say of herself, "It's no great matter."

"…It's a common enough story, I suppose. I was a slave, and Fi alone treated me as a friend."

Sensing the mood, Chlammy continued so as to divert the course of the conversation.

"But to treat a slave as a friend could cause a commotion beyond merely tarnishing the family's reputation, so of course, we can't act like that publicly."

"Well, I, for my part, don't like it one little *bit*."

As Fi bubbled up fluffily but with a hint of anger, Chlammy continued.

"The Nirvalen family is known in Elven Gard. Its name has

graced the lower seats of the upper house of legislature for many generations, and since its previous head passed away last year, Fi has become the de facto head—"

Then the one who understood the meaning behind her tale and reacted was none other than—

"...Then Fiel is an acting member of the Upper House—wait, f-for a member of the Upper House to plot a movement to free the slaves—is that not treason?!"

—That would be an unheard-of scandal in the greatest country in the world. But, *rather than trifles like that*, everyone's gazes now descended on Steph with looks of astonishment.

"—S-Steph, you actually followed our conversation?! Are you sick again? Do you have a fever?!"

At Sora, who verbalized what everyone was thinking, Steph followed on her existing momentum to turn around and shout:

"Can you please remove the label of *idiot* you have placed upon me? Were I not more knowledgeable about politics than a certain *two monarchs* who cast all business of national administration upon me, I should scarcely serve the purpose!"

W-well, setting aside the incredible spectacle unfolded before their eyes. Sora looked into Fi's eyes and asked:

"...Is that all right with you, Fi?"

"Paardon? What do you meaan?"

"Working with us may lead to the downfall of Elven Gard, you know?"

—Yes, as Chlammy had mentioned, what Sora was plotting involved the Eastern Union, and *beyond that*—but.

"Ahh, but that time will come when it coomes."

Fi, with her same sunny smile.

"I don't really care, as long as Chlammy doesn't get hurt... The family and such, frankly, doesn't really matter to me... And I've had such an earful of the old councillors, if possible, I would like to be rid of the headship..."

With her gentle smile, as ungraspable as the snow.

"In fact, at times I have even thought it would be simpler if the state itself were to disappeaar, eh-heh-heh!"

"Wh-what shocking statements you make so offhandedly..."

Steph took a step back at the words produced by that smile.

...So she was saying that she wouldn't mind destroying her homeland as long as it was for Chlammy's sake. Under normal circumstances, one would have to suspect such words...but Sora felt that—perhaps because he had received some of Chlammy's memories—Sora felt that her words were free of falsehood. When he compared the relationship of the two...with his with Shiro—a strange sympathy emerged.

"If I take my eyes off Chlammy, why, she'll go crying in a corner, so I'd like to stay by her side."

Fi spoke while stroking Chlammy fondly, to which Chlammy replied:

"I-I don't cry! I've never cried!"

"Uh, what about when we beat you to become monarch and you were sobbing like a—"

Sora's correction promptly received the evil eye from Chlammy, whom Fi kept stroking.

"Ahh, just as I thooought; I'm always saying Chlammy gets carried awayy."

Resentfully, but not making to sweep away her hand, Chlammy vociferated.

"I-I said I didn't cry, all right? J-just because you've known me since I was an infant, could you please not go on treating me as you would a child?!"

Watching this, Sora quietly remembered, from Chlammy's memory, Fiel's age. She looked in her early teens, but, being an Elf or whatever, in fact—she was *fifty-two*. And at Fiel's smile as she went on stroking Chlammy with no sign of satiation, Sora thought:

(—Not a friend so much as a mom...yeah.) Thus, as if bearing witness to something *unknown*, with a slight sense of envy, Sora and Shiro looked on...

■■■

"Well, then! We've shared our minds; now, to further deepen our acquaintance—"

"I'm not getting in the bath with you."

"H-how did you know?!"

Sora dismayed at having had his thoughts read like that. Chlammy looked back at him in exasperation and sighed.

"Has this man forgotten he gave me all his memories?"

"Mgh—mghghh!"

Curses, this was a most problematic situation. In this world—the *procurement of pr0n* was an issue of the most pressing nature! And now that they even had an Elf girl, Fiel—how could he miss this! As Sora instantly tried to come up with a strategy, help arrived from an unexpected source.

"Chlammy, it's imporrtant to get to know the people you're fighting wiith."

"Hwough?!"

At Fi's words, who she thought was her friend, Chlammy's mask dropped.

"Why, you told me to get along with Jibril, didn't youu?"

"Wh-what does that have to do with us all going into the bath and being photographed!"

But Sora, as if this was it, mobilized every one of his gray matter cells. Sora's ghost whispered that, though he knew not Fi's intent, he had to take this opportunity.

"In the world we come from, there is a traditional Japanese practice to deepen friendship—through 'naked communion.'"

Sora spoke boldly, and Chlammy pounced back.

"Wh-when have you ever used a bath for that purpose since coming to this world!"

For Chlammy, who possessed Sora's memories, it was easy to point this out. It was a matter of course; Sora had never even thought of such a thing. It was a given that Chlammy should question him. But, yet—it was still possible to conquer this debate!

"Well, see, Steph and Jibril have both effectively been bound to me by the Covenants. But, in this case, we're having you help us based on a relationship of trust. Now we can only rely on traditional culture—Jibril, if you would."

"I am here."

Sora snapped his fingers, Jibril gliding to her knees beside him.

"Faithful vassal, will you use this tablet to explain to them the great Japanese tradition of 'naked communion'?"

Accurately digesting Sora's intent, Jibril manipulated the tablet.

"Ahem—'naked communion' takes its roots in an ancient ritual dating back to the Warring States period in Japan, in which participants displayed to each other that they had no hidden weapons and exposed their bodies to reveal their abilities, so as to lay their hands open and to prove to each other their good faith."

On Jibril's effortless fabrication of a text written nowhere, Chlammy nonetheless harped all the more.

"Y-you lie! There's no such story in Sora's memory!"

"Yeah, I didn't know about its roots myself. But you should be able to find a memory that it deepens trust?"

A moment's pause. Probably rummaging through Sora's memories—and then.

"—All I see are lascivious memories outnumbering such things entirelyyy?!"

Chlammy, presumably flooded with sex tidbits and erotic videos, turned beet-red and screamed. Apparently unable after all to sit and watch this, Fi intervened.

"All righht, Chlammy. Allow me to speak up on your behalf."

"H-wha? Uh, o-okay—thank—"

"Sir, I'm sure you must have realized this yourseelf, but what Chlammy is trying to say is thiis. She's no confidence in her body, so she'd rather—"

"I—I-I-I-I-I-I'm trying to say no such thing!!"

Fi, wide-eyed and vacant.

"You're *not*? But..."

Fi's eyes glanced around. At Jibril's. Steph's. And then her own bosom. And, finally, Chlammy's...chest. With eyes full of compassion.

"Why, worry not, Chlammy. A woman's value is not in her chest, you know!!"

"—Uh, uh...f-fine, already! I'll go!"

Chlammy, pointing ferociously at Shiro.

"D-do you think I would have such a reason in the presence of a tiny girl such as this?"

Shiro, pointed to, lifted her eyes from her DSP and tilted her head. But Fi, with a yet deeper gentle smile, in the manner of a mother teaching her child.

"Chlammy, to compare yourself to a chiild is just humiliating yourself too much."

Chlammy slammed her hands onto the table and stood up.

...On the verge of tears.

"Fi, I hate you! I-I don't care; where's the bath?!"

"Now, then, I shall escort you *all*!"

Immediately, Jibril, with bath sundries for each of them, who knows when she picked them up.

"...I'm getting in, too, am I; yes, well, this was known to me?"

...And so, watching Chlammy and Steph being taken away by Jibril. Sora, holding Shiro, got up himself and asked Fi, who was likewise stepping forth to follow.

"—So, why'd you play along with my bullshit?"

"What, you mean it was untrue? Why, how *abominable*."

Fi still smiled as she bullshitted right back. But, to Sora and Shiro's probing silence as they walked alongside, Fi responded.

"...If everyone undresses themseelves, then I can analyze their personalities to some extent from the spiritual activity in their bodiees, and if I can grasp *the probability they'll cut me in my sleep*, it makes it easier to deal wiiith."

"I see," chuckled Sora. "So you do want naked communion, just like Jibril said."

With her usual fluffy and, yes—*ungraspable* smile, Fi continued.

"The memories you gave to Chlammy have caused her to trust you unconditionally. I have no way of knowing their contents, and I am truly grateful that you did not take our lives—but."

Still smiling, Fi narrowed her eyes.

"You should not assuume that if Chlammy trusts you, then I trust you."

Her slightly open eyes spoke—if this too was a trick. Then she would use any means at her disposal to *wipe Sora & co. from the land*, taking all of Elkia with them. Yet brushing off her gaze, Sora answered with a smile.

"You're right on. If you were dumb enough to trust a trickster when he says, 'Trust me,' then that would be a problem for me, too."

Falling silent while still smiling, Sora and Shiro, walking together, with Fi. Suddenly, Sora asked.

"Hey, let me ask—do all Elves have wits as quick as yours?"

Laughing softly at his question, Fi answered.

"If I knew that, then I'd know just how far up my *treason* is known."

—She had, after all, even considered *the possibility someone was turning a blind eye.*

"Ha-ha, looks like Elven Gard may be our last enemy after all."

"So long as you do not hurt Chlammy, then I shall help you with all my strength."

—As long as they didn't hurt Chlammy, she didn't mind if they destroyed Elven Gard. Tacitly but clearly saying this, Fi.

"Now, sir, in consideration of the preparation of the kindling, it is time I go to Chlammy's side."

Watching Fi as she caught up to Chlammy with steps with a sense of softness, Sora muttered aside.

"—Jibril."

"I am here."

Hearing Sora's faint murmur and instantly shifting to appear at his back, Jibril spoke.

"...Did she use some kind of magic?"

"No, there was no response whatsoever."

At this answer, Shiro frowned slightly.

—It was discomfort at the appearance that someone had read *her brother three or four moves ahead*, at which even she had yet to arrive. And Sora, too, laughed a bit regretfully, scratching his head.

"She can see through to my *true intent* without using magic? If that's the case, then that damages my confidence a little."

If he lost to a user of übermagic tricks in cunning and mind games, then he'd really be screwed. Had Fi actually read all the way to the *last move* he'd prepared?

"…Oh, well, eventually we'll be facing Elven Gard, too; we might as well get a look at their skills."

■■■

—Now of course, quite a bit of firewood had been burned in consideration of age-appropriateness. But behind the shroud of steam all that fire had created lay, undoubtedly, *paraíso*. Paradise. In the bath chamber sat a pouting Shiro. Though things had been improved somewhat by the mysterious shampoo "specially formulated with spirit water" that Jibril had brought, still it seemed she did not like baths. Steph all the same washed Shiro's hair, then did a double-take as Chlammy entered.

"Wha, Chlammy, you had a figure like that?"

"Hmph, I'm the type who looks more slender in clothes…"

For having been picked on so much about her figure, Steph was astonished to see that Chlammy had a shape as ideal as a model's. Jibril and Fi were supposed to be present, too. Yes, supposed to be… And considering this was a bath—obviously, without a shred of clothing. However, Sora, clothed, and with his back to them had no way of verifying any of this. *(Please…oh cameras on our phones and tablet. I believe in you!)* The cameras had been set up at three strategic points so as to avoid the ban flag from recording a naked minor—Shiro. Suddenly, Sora, praying that this time his cameras might take a perfect shot while he suppressed his urge to turn, heard himself addressed.

"...Master, did you expect this?"

Snapped from his reveries by Jibril behind him, Sora responded in the affirmative.

"Of course."

Unable to turn around (*oh, well*)—Sora called at his back instead.

"Fi... Uh, I mean, Fiel, Your Ladyship?"

"Ohh? What's this all of a sudden, acting all formal."

At Fi's reply, seemingly quite near him, apparently, Sora continued.

"*The spell you're using to disguise Chlammy's boobs*, is it an illusion? Or are you actually transforming them?"

"Why, I am transforming them, but now that you say that—"

Still smiling, Fi called.

"Chlammy, the game's up, and anyway, I think disguise is a bit discourteous in naked commuunion."

With a sound like that of a cork popping from a bottle, the magic was dispelled and, back to her original shape—the flat-chested Chlammy.

"Don't admit it so easily, Fi! If you're going to do this, you shouldn't have done anything to begin with!"

For some reason strangely sympathizing with her cruel predicament, Steph intervened.

"...It's all right. If you hold your head high, there will be good things."

"Don't look at me like that! They'll get bigger!"

Chlammy misinterpreted Steph's comfort as about her breasts; Fi resumed regardless.

"So, what kind of magic is it that you desire?"

"Mm—glad we could get to the point."

With Fi accurately grasping his intent, Sora nodded grandly and spoke.

"—It is possible you could make me female?!"

The verve transmitted beyond the back of the shouting man. Shook the pervading steam mightily, as if summoning a divine wind...

"If only I had this, I could view the paradise unfolding behind my back! If I were the same sex, no matter how anyone looked at it, it would be entirely wholesome! If that were R-18, then public baths and hot springs, too, would be R-18! It would be perfectly, invincibly wholesome!"

"If the lechery that swirls in your heart is the same, I think fundamentally it would be the same."

"There is no physical evidence by which you can prove what is in my heart!"

"How fantastic, Master! I am overwhelmed with emotion at your unhesitating willingness to so boldly carry forth with such absurd reasoning!!"

And then, Fi told him.

"It is possible, I suppose."

"Are you serious?!"

The sheer effort, by dint of his reason, required to repress his spinal reflex to turn threatened to give Sora back pain. Ohhh… Ohh, a goddess was before him—no, behind him!

"However, you cannot turn back, but do you mind?"

—Wha?

"There are two magical elements that determine your seex. If you have two of the same element, then you are female; if they are different, you are male; by magic, it is possible to make you female by making the elements the saame; however, I'm unable to turn you baaack."

…Why, after coming to a fantasy world, was he still being lectured about X and Y chromosomes? Shiro, her hair being washed by Steph, answered for him.

"…No, thanks…"

Sora, looking up at the ceiling—no, at the invisible sky, cried unmanly tears.

"Come on now, fantasy… In a world with covenants and magic, how can you not just change someone's goddamn sex! Get off your ass, stupid world; put some effort into it!!"

Though Sora cried out, all he could do now was to paint the heavenly expanse behind him in his mind. And leave it all to the power of man's toil by the sweat of his brow—trusting in the science of the three cameras…

■■■

Elkia Royal Castle—the library. Sora and Shiro had apparently come here directly after getting out of the bath. Shiro, with her wet hair still wrapped in a towel, was intently hammering away some scrawl on the blackboard. Beside her, Sora was fiddling with the tablet while drawing lines on countless sheets of paper. The sun starting to go down, all that illuminated the room was the flame of flickering candles and Sora's tablet. The clownish atmosphere present just a moment ago—was now nowhere to be found in their serious faces.

"—…"

Having thought to say something before she went home, Chlammy stood still. Countless sheets of paper were strewn about the room, some scratched out, some Xed. The meaning of the array of symbols being bashed on the board, of the countless lines being drawn by Sora, was not entirely comprehensible to her even with the gift of Sora's memory. However—she had an idea. After one deep breath, Chlammy stepped into the room.

"…Is this *your strategy to vanquish the Eastern Union*?"

"Mm, sorry, don't talk to Shiro—well, I guess even if you do she won't notice."

As if she'd not even noticed them talking. Shiro, unblinking, went on scratching countless equations onto the board, very much like a machine.

"Eh, frankly this is Shiro's field. I've got no clue; I'm just acting as an assistant."

What Sora was drawing with his right hand looked to Chlammy clearly like strategic maps. However, what he was looking at on the tablet he manipulated with his left hand—

"You ask why I am reviewing the footage from the bath just now?"

"...If you're expecting a reaction like Stephanie Dola's from me, you'll be disappointed."

"Not too convincing when you're blushing and covering your breasts."

—Forget it, she had been wrong to expect to have a meaningful conversation with this man. As Chlammy turned away with these thoughts, Sora's voice stopped her.

"You came to ask if we can really win, right?"

—Chlammy was reminded how distasteful she found this man. He seemed to have developed a habit of breaking others' strides. This was clear already from the memories she had received—but all the more for that. There was one thing that weighed on her.

"—Yes, that is right."

"You know the answer, don't you? You have my memories."

"They don't explain everything."

Yes, she still couldn't understand. The strategy Sora and Shiro had developed together was, indeed, a splendid work, a humbling feat. But—no matter how she looked at it, *there was a flaw.* And yet Sora, knowing that flaw—had come to the conclusion that there was *no problem.* No matter where she looked in Sora's memories, she could not find a basis for the *confidence* that made him so sure.

"It is certainly possible in theory. But theory is one thing—"

There was a common observation she could make about the chess game they'd played with her and the Othello match—no. About the whole range of games Sora remembered ever playing—which was.

"*If you make one wrong step, you'll be at the bottom of the gorge,* won't you. How do you call that 'unbeatable'?"

—Yes, so many matches decorated in victory in Sora's memory. But all of them were built on too dangerous a tightrope. How could this be called "unbeatable"? But then Sora spoke, looking back at Chlammy as if sincerely taken by surprise.

"It's not unbeatable if we make one wrong step. That's why we have to *not make one wrong step*, right?"

* * *

—This was it. No matter how hard she searched through Sora's memories, she couldn't find the basis for this claim.

"How can you be sure you won't make a single mistake?"

While Chlammy addressed him glaringly, Sora still answered with a laugh.

"Ha-ha-ha, well, that's impossible. If it were just me, I'd definitely screw it up...but—"

Fffft. Sora's eyes shifted, and she followed them—to the white genius. Fiercely bashing more equations onto the board, the white, white, eleven-year-old girl.

"—Blank is a different story. Even if I misstep, there's Shiro."

The phrase that filled Sora's memories—" " *doesn't lose*. Chlammy, having come this far, finally realized a fact she'd overlooked. The Othello game they'd played for each other's existence. The last three pieces she'd been unable to take—three elements that were more important than his very being. Now she had a feeling she knew what they governed.

(...I see. It's because *I only have the memories of Sora individually* that it doesn't look unbeatable...that explains it.) The existence of a sister he valued more than his own existence—Shiro. If that was what made him say that the two-in-one gamer's strategy, though it seemed like walking out from a cliff balancing on a cotton string, was unbeatable. Then she, who had failed to take that *trust* from him—could never understand his confidence. But the countless words Sora had spoken to Shiro. And the countless words he had told himself.

"—You...found your wings, didn't you."

"Mm?"

And, imitating Sora, Chlammy grinned and spoke.

"—'Hey, Shiro, they say people can change, but is that really true'...huh."

"Wha—?!"

—There it was. She'd wanted to see his expression. Thus, Chlammy smiled contentedly at the blushing Sora and turned away.

"It's pretty embarrassing, but I must say I respect that way of thinking. Why don't you take pride in it?"

"Shut up!"

"Must be tough to have such a good sister. *Leaves you with something to prove, doesn't it*—dear—big—bro-ther. ♥"

"Look, you—just go home already! People are gonna get suspicious if you stick around in Elkia too long!"

As she left, many things went through Chlammy's head. But she decided not to say them. Instead, she turned—and left one short comment.

"—I believe…in 'human potential.'"

The words that returned were sullen, yet strong.

"No shit. You're human, too."

Closing her eyes at these words, Chlammy left Elkia's castle.

CHAPTER 3 KILLING GIANTS

INDUCTION

Elkia Royal Castle—Presence Chamber. The two monarchs of Immanity resting on the throne, sprawled out as if melting.

"Hey, this is frickin' weak... When the hell is the Eastern Union planning to tell us when our game is?"

"...So, bored..."

Already almost five days had passed since their exchange with Chlammy and Fiel. After getting their groove on like that, now they were being made to wait until they lost it entirely. Even Steph, usually in the position of chastising them, could say nothing. In the back of the mind of the nervous-looking Steph, a certain possibility flashed.

"C-could it be they've forgotten—or we haven't got their letter... perhaps?"

—At Steph, who spoke remembering that previously the letters they had been sending had never arrived. The melted Sora picked himself up and formed a grin more sadistic than ever before.

"...Ohh? If that's the case, then someone's gonna have to be taught a little lesson—ya know?"

In the back of his mind spinning history's greatest prank, which he'd saved as his *final trump card*—

"Master, I'm sorry to intrude."

Jibril apologized, appearing from thin air. Their gazes locked on the cylinder in her hand. Sora and Shiro sat up violently.

"Whoa, Jibril! Is that what I—?"

"Yes, it is a letter from the Eastern Union, indicating their acceptance of the game and the appointed date."

Beaming, Jibril continued.

"It seems it was being suppressed within the Elkia Royal Castle so as to stop the game with the Eastern Union. You see, there was a fellow who started acting suspiciously each time he witnessed me—"

"Uh... You didn't..."

This was Jibril. She couldn't have killed—

"Please be at ease. I persuaded him in the most courteous and peaceful manner. Simply looking gently into his eyes and admonishing him lightly was enough for him to moisten his lower body, weep, sob, tell me everything I needed to know, and give me the letter."

"I-I see..."

—The Ten Covenants didn't cover intimidation, huh? Wait but, then, wouldn't withholding the letter from them amount to plunder or— But Steph said, holding her head:

"...I should have known... After all, Immanity's life is at stake... Someone in the government who hadn't taken part in the covenant not to make false reports would still have been able to use a game to lift someone's right to deliver the letter and—"

...Huh, so Steph really did have a head for politics. Secretly thinking to himself that he should raise his estimation of Steph a bit, Sora continued.

"—*It wasn't specified when they had to deliver it*, I guess. Hey, Immanity, you're pretty sneaky when it comes to things like this. I wish you'd just use those brains for something more useful to the country."

"For now, you are the enemy of Immanity. I think they are applying them perfectly?"

Steph's sarcastic reply passed epically over Sora's head.

"Let's seee, then, what does it————Hey, Shiro, what's today's date?"

"...Twenty-seventh."

Strained-faced Sora's confirmation was answered immediately by Shiro.

"—D00d, that's today; today's supposed to be the game!"

"Huh?! Uh, um, what time—"

To a flustered Steph, Sora howled.

"Starting in the evening—we don't even have half a day! Come on, everyone get ready fast!"

"A-all r—"

"Your humble servant Jibril is ready anytime."

"...I'm...all, good..."

"And her brother, Sora, is also all clear to go anytime! So all of you, let's go!"

That Sora and his crew were prepared for takeoff just by standing up stressed Steph out.

"E-excuse me! Look, th-this is an official battle of nations! At least you need to dress—"

"What? This is my official regalia. You got a problem with that?"

Perhaps it was the way of the world that a normal person among weirdos would always be called the weirdo. The three stared at Steph as if to ask, *What are you on?* to which she replied—

"—F-fine! Very well, we'll go as we are!"

"And so, Masters and little Dora, please clutch onto me. We shall shift to the embassy—"

"Oh, Jibril, nope."

Refusing the maximum-speed mode of transport proffered by Jibril and turning to face Steph, Sora ordered:

"Steph, prepare a carriage at the *front* of the castle—we're gonna go out in style, from the frickin' *front*."

As Jibril failed to grasp the meaning of his suggestion, Steph was dumbfounded.

"Wha… D-do you realize there's a riot out there?!"

"*That's why*—look. Why do you think I *started* this riot?"

■■■

The grand square before the Elkia Royal Castle, mobbed by demonstrators, a hurricane of invective. Before it, the enormous main gate of Elkia Royal Castle slowly opened with thunderous noise. The rally was ready to launch a barrage of bile upon whosoever should appear—but. At the four who stepped out, silence fell.

At the steps of the four, the crowd in the square, draped in stillness, parted and made way. Walking at the center with black hair and dark eyes as deep and cold as night was the king—Sora. At his right, with eyes more bewitchingly ruby-red than ever before, the queen—Shiro. Walking a step behind, with amber eyes twinkling quietly, their servant—Jibril. Each of their eyes with their own glow, each filled with an uncommon resolve and a confidence that seemed absolute—that forbade the people to form words.

…Well, that's overromanticizing it a little. Mainly it was *Jibril's gaze and placid smile* that said it: If you would like to disparage my master, please feel free to do so in exchange for your life. Her overwhelming presence stopped people from even breathing and stole all words from the crowd. Far behind, aquamarine-eyed Steph awkwardly scurried to catch up.

—In the end, the steps of Sora and his companions allowed not a single word of abuse.

Steph, having clambered onto the carriage, out of breath, interrogated Sora as she caught her breath.

"Y-you *started* the riot—what do you mean?"

But Sora said to Shiro as if the query was unexpected.

"Huh, Shiro didn't explain?"

"...?"

As Shiro tilted her head, Sora realized just as he'd said it.

...It was a stupid question. There was no way Shiro would take the initiative to explain something to one other than Sora.

"Ohh, it's like. When I bet the Immanity Piece, I was aiming for—three things."

Sora raised three fingers and turned to face Steph.

"One, it goes without saying, was to drag the Eastern Union into the game. Another, which you probably know, was to lure in Chlammy and draw her to our side. And then the third—"

Sora, having counted down to his last finger, smiled mischievously.

"—was the *distrustful eyes of the masses.*"

"Huh...?"

"Who needs a bunch of suckers who just trust that we're definitely gonna win? What we need is a bunch of assholes who are going to watch the match with bloodshot eyes, wondering if we're gonna throw it. Effectively, what this will do is to prevent the Eastern Union from cheating blatantly. There's no spectator you can trust more than one who doesn't trust you."

Sora grinned gleefully. Disregarding Steph's bewilderment, he called to the coachman with abandon.

"So get that carriage out. Our destination—Izzy's house!

"...Onward!"

■■■

At the outskirts of the capital, Elkia, a towering, giant building positioned just on this side of the border. The embassy of the Eastern Union in Elkia. As Sora's party got out of the carriage, they were greeted by an aging, white-haired Werebeast in garb resembling Japanese formal wear. The deputy ambassador of the Eastern Union in Elkia—Ino Hatsuse.

"...We have been awaiting your arrival."

"Dude, you're the ones who made us wait. Come on, you ready for this?"

Despite Sora talking smack the moment he got down from the carriage, Ino seemed nonetheless to take caution as he answered briefly.

"...Please, right this way."

Guided into the building—the embassy—Sora's party walked behind Ino, who said nothing.

"Hey, the old guy's pretty reticent, isn't he. What's his deal?"

To Sora as he muttered, the guy knew how to get smart with us before. Steph answered with a tired face.

"After you swindled him into betting the entire continental territory of the Eastern Union, that's what you have to say?

"For heaven's sake—," said Steph, holding her head. "To be so carefree right before a game played with the *Immanity Piece* at stake, aren't you the ones who have something wrong with you?"

Jibril scanned the scene giddily (despite this being their second time here), practically drooling in fascination at everything she saw. In contrast, Shiro yawned softly, messing with her phone, while Sora folded his arms behind his head and yammered flightily. Meanwhile, Steph desperately tried to suppress the pain in her stomach.

"You okay there, Steph? Relax your shoulders. You're never gonna be able to keep it up like that."

"Thank you for your concern. However, the cause of my stomachaches, in 100 percent of cases, is you two..."

They were led to the same reception chamber as before.

"...If you will, please wait here for a bit until the appointed time for the game."

"Sure thing. And make sure you let in all our spectators, just like we said, okay?"

Upon Ino's single bow and wordless departure, Sora spoke as he unhesitatingly stretched out on the sofa.

"So, Jibril, wake me up when it's time."

"Your wish is my command. Please enjoy your rest."

"...Me, too."

...and, on the stomach of the supine Sora, Shiro unhesitatingly curled up and closed her eyes. Within only a few seconds, the siblings were breathing with the comfortable sounds of slumber.

"...I cannot believe this. What kind of sense do they have?"

In a few short hours would begin a match that would determine the fate of all humans. Given that Steph had been fighting nausea and stomachache since the moment she'd been informed of the game schedule, Jibril, seemingly as at ease as Sora and Shiro, suggested:

"Dora, why don't you get some rest as well? According to my masters' literature, the Immanity brain is at its peak function in the few hours after rising?"

"If I had the nerves of steel to sleep in this situation, I'd like to—"

"I understand. Things must be difficult if my masters consider it *necessary to do so*."

"......!"

These words made Steph's face contort.

"It appears that this game *demands the full capacity* of even my masters. Should this be the case, I suppose I shall have to take it a bit seriously as well."

Steph felt her stomachache get even worse. And so—for Steph, the few hours until the start of the game passed as a series of trips between the restroom and the reception room.

■■■

"...*Yawn*... Oh, Steph. Looks like you've lost weight in the last few hours?"

"*Grown haggard*, I think is the phrase that might apply..."

Approaching the game's appointed start time, an exhausted Steph answered a freshly risen Sora.

"Great. Shiro, how you feeling?"

"...All, green."

Shiro answered Sora's question with eyes glowing several degrees brighter than usual.

"You, Jibril?"

"A Flügel's condition knows no variance. I am always ready to devote all my spirits at your command."

Yet even Jibril answered with a restless expression swept clean of her usual laxity.

"Steph—well...yeah, I guess there's no hope there."

With that, Sora spoke slowly.

"By the way, Steph, you remember the game we played the other day?"

"...Which game do you mean?"

"The game where we guessed when the pigeon would fly off."

"Oh, yes...the day you turned me into a dog; what of it, Sir?"

"You remember how we made that wager, and I—*still haven't specified what I want*?"

"—Huh?"

"Jibril, can you make it so the Werebeasts can't hear us here?"

"Certainly, Master; I shall envelop you and little Dora in spirits so that sound cannot escape."

Jibril nodding once, revolving her halo. Sora turned back to Steph.

"'Kay, Steph, now I'm gonna perform a *very special charm* on you..."

With a very, very sweet smile, but approaching rather creepily, Sora inspired in Steph only the worst of expectations—

■■■

—The game's appointed start time. Shown in by Ino, the party arrived at one floor of the embassy. The vast, right-angled hall gave the impression of taking up the entire story of the massive building. A single giant screen filled each wall, across all four sides of the floor. Amidst this, come to watch the game that would determine the fate of the human race, crowded several hundred—no, perhaps even a thousand Immanities, watching the stage with looks full of suspicion. On the stage, before the front screen, was a black box—and upon it were situated five chairs.

"......"

Demurely seated in one of those chairs waited their opponent. Ambassador of the Eastern Union in Elkia. A black-haired Werebeast with ears as long as those of a fennec fox—Izuna Hatsuse. With her eyes closed as if focusing her mind, the girl showed no trace of the warmth she had exhibited the other day.

"...If you'll each be seated here, please."

At Ino's urging, Sora sat next to Izuna. Then, in order to the right, Shiro, Jibril, and Steph followed. Having checked that they were seated, Ino, standing beside Izuna, read from the document he held.

"Now—if you will, the review of the covenant shall commence."

Someone could be heard to swallow.

"The Eastern Union wagers all it possesses on the continent of Lucia. The Kingdom of Elkia wagers its Race Piece—in other words, all rights, all territory, and everything else possessed by Immanity. Under these conditions, a game specified by the Eastern Union shall be played by a total of five players, comprising the representative of the Eastern Union as well as the two monarchs of the Kingdom of Elkia and their two attendants—*one on four.*"

Seeing that all of his demands—including that it be *one on four*—had gone through, Sora smirked.

—Of course they had. They *hadn't given them a choice.*

"Moreover, per the Eastern Union's standard practice, a concomitant demand shall be made that all memories of the game be forgotten. This demand applies to all Immanities including the players and spectators."

Ino continued neutrally.

"Also, the rules shall be explained *after the game begins*. Therefore, should the game be refused after hearing the rules, the match shall be ruled invalid, and the memories regarding the rules shall be forgotten solely—is this truly acceptable?"

—It was bullshit. You wouldn't find out what the game was until after you bet? And then he spelled out what a heavy demand it was and bothered to ask, "Is this truly acceptable?" *Acceptable, my ass*, was the collective thought of all in the audience. But, responding all too carefreely:

"Sure, *no problem*. But I just want to clarify two things."

Eagerly, the king of Immanity—Sora.

"Even if we withdraw, all that we're gonna lose are our memories of today's game. If you're hoping you can make us quit by hitting us with an *impossible game* and then take *all our memories*, forget it. Don't waste your time."

Then, peering deeper into Ino's eyes.

"And here's the second thing. 'If cheating is discovered in a game, it shall be counted as a loss'—as long as you're not forgetting this fundamental premise of the Ten Covenants, there's *no problem*. Come, then, let's get started."

...At Sora, who so easily—too easily—struck down *one of the traps* laid by the upper brass of the Eastern Union. At Sora, who seemed not to consider in the slightest the possibility that he might lose. At his actions, which appeared to onlookers unsurpassably rash. Even Ino and Izuna, who *knew that the game had been laid bare*. All grimaced for different reasons.

"...Then, taking this as a sign of agreement—let us declare the covenant."

At Ino's announcement, Sora and Shiro raised their hands. Jibril, unhesitatingly, and Steph, hesitantly.

"*Aschente*."

"*Aschente*, please."

The agent plenipotentiary of Immanity, Sora and Shiro, and each of the players. And the agent plenipotentiary of the Eastern Union, Izuna Hatsuse.

—Each pronounced to one another the word of oath under the Ten Covenants.

* * *

“Okay, Shiro, don’t let go of my hand, all right?”

“...You too, Brother.”

As they gripped each other’s hands, Sora leaned back in his chair and said:

“Come—let’s begin the game.”

“...Very well, I shall do the honors.”

Ino, thus muttering, manipulated the black box—probably turning on the power. The giant screens covering the walls lit up.

—This was it: the game for the human race itself. And for the entire continental domain of the third largest country in the world. Amidst a whirlpool of countless emotions: tension, doubt, despair. The hall was crammed with as many as a thousand spectators yet went as silent as the bottom of the sea. Beside Izuna, viewing the screen, Sora spoke.

“Hey, Izuna.”

“—What, please?”

Words from the enemy just before the start of the game. For a moment, she doubted whether she should respond to them. But his query, delivered as he faced the screen without any special excitement or emotion—

—were words Izuna would come to regret having asked for.

“When’s the last time you felt a game was fun?”

Before Izuna could process the question, the display went black, and—

—their consciousness was swallowed into the screen.

■■■

As his consciousness dived, still Sora considered calmly. (We’ve found out the game from the info the old king left us and the intel we've gathered.) It was, indeed, a *video game*, just as Sora had uncovered. The one discrepancy was that this game was taking place virtually, with a *full-consciousness dive*. The previous king had written that "it takes place in another world," but that must have been as far as he'd understood.

(At the time, he was playing Ino Hatsuse. The old dude.) It was written that the game was a "shooting game"—in other words, an FPS. But now that time had gone by since the last game, the role of the player had been handed down to Izuna Hatsuse. It was probably safe to assume that the game itself had changed…*but*— (Considering the properties of Werebeast, the cheats they're likely to use, and the fact that this is a *public match* under the eyes of spectators, we can also assume that they're not gonna change the fundamental type of game.) Indeed, *under these conditions*. No other genre could be imagined to provide Werebeast with "certain victory." (But they are gonna mess with the detailed rules, change up the map, definitely. This is a game of how we're gonna respond quickly to things we expected and things we didn't and adapt our strategy—) But as loading finished and the world assembled before his eyes, Sora's thoughts crashed, and his eyes opened to their maximum. It was——

"————No, way."

"……——"

The siblings cursed their folly. They'd anticipated countless rule sets, countless maps, and prepared countless strategies. But—this was the one map they hadn't thought of at all. It definitely was. They knew it…they'd never thought to see it again. Oh, that dear and dreadful place, so chock-full of their trauma—

There was no mistaking it if they tried—it was *Tokyo, Japan*.

"…Sorry, Steph, Jibril."

"Uh, what?"

"——*Hh!* Ah, eh, did you call?!"

To Steph, spacing out, and Jibril, drooling at the unfamiliar scenery, Sora spoke.

"We can't do this. Sorry, Immanity is done for."

"Chatter chatter shiver shiver"

"Huh...wh-what now?! After you said all that—"

"Sorry forgive me I never even considered it might be in Tokyo we can't do this our home field is not to our advantage we're no more use so I really apologize but you'll just have to figure something out—"

"Chatter chatter shiver shiver"

As the brother blathered away with his eyes rolling back in his head and the sister crouched and trembled with her head in her hands, Jibril stuttered.

"—Do—do you mean to say this is your world?"

Then the narrator's—rather Ino's—voice resounded.

"Was it a shock? Welcome to the game world."

"...Game...world."

"Indeed. This is the setting of the game. The game will take place in this fictional—"

"Wait."

"—Yes?"

"Let me check. You said—it's *fictional, a place that doesn't exist,* right?"

"Yes. Is this a problem?"

Looking around at the signs, Sora checked objectively. Crowded in countless glass-sided buildings, a world built out of asphalt and concrete.

...Indeed, it looked quite like downtown Tokyo—but. The signs dotted around clearly were not in Japanese, and there were shrine gates here and there, more of a sense of nature... Looking carefully, it wasn't exactly the Tokyo Sora knew.

I ♥ 人類

"—So you're saying this is an artificial virtual world that you guys *imagined and created?*"

"Yes. How quick is your understanding."

"——Shiiiiiiiiiiiiiit, don't troll us like that!"

Sora's mighty roar echoed throughout the game's "Tokyo."

"—Aaaah, shit! You just triggered goddamn flashbacks! I almost ripped out my arteries... Don't make such confusing crap, you damn old fart!"

At the wildly raging Sora, Ino's confusion only increased.

"...What is it that angers you so...? Are you dissatisfied with this stage?"

"I'm dripping with dissatisfaction! What possessed you to use this stage?! What is this, psychological warfare or griefing?"

"Sir... It is simply because the young of late have become enamored of science fiction stages *such as this. There is no deep intent."*

"Uh...uhh? Science...fiction?"

—O-oh. Calm down. You gotta calm down, Sora, virgin, eighteen. This is a world that has elves and dragons—just like we all imagined them in our old world. Just like Disboard is fantasy in our world. For these guys, a world like present-day Earth is the product of fancy—that's all it is. This is a game our consciousness has dived into; it's a fictional world; it's not Tokyo. Sora breathed deeply, reassuring himself.

"*Hhh...Hhh...* Okay, I'm good. I'm calm now."

"*...Chatter chatter shiver shiver*"

"Shiro, calm down. This isn't Tokyo. It just looks like it. It's an imaginary place they made up."

"......*Hig*...uh?"

Perhaps just too traumatized. Shiro apparently hadn't even heard what Ino said until Sora repeated it to her.

"Yeah, it's just a game anyway. We can walk around if it's in a game, right, like *Pe*sona* or *Ste*ns;Gate* or *Akiba's *rip*. We're inside a game. It's okay inside a game. And offline we've still got a good grip on each other's hand. Right, yeah?"

"...In a, game...mm...hmm, o...kay..."

With eyes still somewhat vacant, Shiro got up.

"Ehh, well, with that—shall we proceed with the game?"

—Come to think of it, this game was being observed by the human race. Sora couldn't see them, but, feeling gazes colder than glaciers fixed on him, he cleared his throat.

"A'ight. We're ready. Let's do this."

"Ahem, in that case, let us start with the opening movie."

"Pardon? What is that?"

"Is it necessary?"

Sora and Shiro, long since having adopted a kneeling posture, replied to the doubtful Steph and Jibril.

"If you skip the opening movie, you fail as a gamer. If you will, ladies, shut up, sit tight, and watch."

"...Nod, nod."

Thus urged, Steph and Jibril reluctantly joined their masters in a kneeling position. And in the skies of "Tokyo," a giant screen was projected.

"You are—popular with girls."

...One second into the opening, Sora was already pretty sure this was going to fail as a game. But his pride as a gamer just barely kept his tongue.

"You are so popular with girls from all over the world, you lead a life of constantly being chased... But you yourself, in your heart of hearts, have just one girl—one love of whom you dream."

Projected along with the ridiculous narration. The image of Izuna, dressed up in cute, florid clothes, as if she weren't already angelic enough.

"But even so, surrounded by such masses of temptation, there is only so long your feelings can stay pure—"

A graphic of a figure chased by hordes of animal-girls and hugged once captured.

"Can you fight through the masses of temptation—and deliver your love through to your one and only?!"

Living or Dead Gaiden
Love or Loved 2: Get Her with Your Bullet of Love

—The opening ended. Or, shall we say, it had ended. Sora holding his head as if trying to contain something. Shiro unspeaking. Beside Jibril as she drooled in fascination, Steph stared puzzledly.

"G-Gramps, do you mind?"

They sure picked some game for a contest on which rested the fate of the nation and the human race. To Sora, about to let slip a snide remark (or nine), Ino apologetically pleaded...

"...Please, could you not say anything? Izuna had us make this game because she dislikes gory content."

...You're pretty fairy-tale after all, aren't you, Izzy?

"More importantly, everyone, please look at the boxes at your feet."

As everyone looked toward their feet, now each had a little box there. The kind of box in which you find ammo in an FPS. Opening it up—

"What is this, a *gun?*"

"...Weird...shape."

"The shape does indeed seem to differ significantly from the 'guns' which appear in your literature."

"What is this? How are you supposed to hold it?"

To the siblings, confused at the bizarre shape of the weapon, and to the two who had never seen a gun, Ino continued.

"Now, please let me explain the rules."

Ino proceeded in a monotone as if reading off the instruction manual.

"Please use the gun provided—to shoot the NPC girls who chase you."

"You shoot them?!"

"At times you will shoot them, at times you will bomb them—to make them fall head over heels for you."

"What is this, *Ga*Gun*?!"

"Once they fall head over heels, they will realize the strength of your love and disappear, leaving you with their power of love."

"...Uh, okay."

"The 'Lovey-Dovey Gun' fires the power of love—technically termed Love Power."

Sora looked down at the bizarre gun he had.

"—This is called a Lovey-Dovey Gun?"

"...Lame."

"It is indeed a thoughtless name. The infantile sensibility of this game comes through in spades."

"Excuse me, please, what is a gun?"

"Your team wins if you shoot your 'one and only,' that is, Izuna, with the Lovey-Dovey Gun—Lovey Gun for short."

"...Rrright."

"However, if one of you is shot by Izuna, then her victim will become her 'slave of love.'"

"—Um...can you just say 'turn on you'?"

"In a world in which all girls adore you, except only for your one true love, the object of this game is to get through to her with the power of love and make her fall head over heels with lovey-dovey feelings—so explains the instruction manual."

Ino's implicit assertion being, *This was not my idea*, prompted a—*Hmm, okay*—from Sora. Summing up the rules in his head, he opened his mouth, eyes squinting.

"...This premise pisses me off. Basically you're saying we go around rejecting every girl in sight. What kind of dickhead are we supposed to be?"

So they all had charisma times, like, a million now, right? Get gibbed. Thrust of it was, everyone was hyper-ultra-popular, but for the four on Sora's team, Izuna was their "one and only." For Izuna, though, they were all her "four and only."

"So, basically, Izuna's going for the harem ending with all four of us in love with her while we're each gunning for Izuna alone."

"Well, yes, that is how it's set up."

"...That's, like, what. It's..."

Through a haze of emotions, Sora searched for words.

"I can deal with this 'cause Izzy's a cute animal-girl, but, say if it were you, Gramps? Right now I'd imagine myself logging out, taking a running start, and smashing your eyes with my fingers."

"I can thoroughly appreciate how you feel, but please remember that you were the one who requested that the game be one-on-four."

—Ino reemphasized that they were the ones responsible for this obnoxious premise. But he continued, now rather showing sympathy toward Sora.

"These days only cutesy games like this are popular... When I was young, we were serious—"

—Sora felt oddly moved to see that there were retro posers in every world.

"...Okay, sure. I want to confirm the rules, so let me ask you a few, Gramps."

"Please ask anything you like."

1. Firing your Lovey Gun or Lovey Bombs uses up Love Power.
2. You can replenish Love Power by shooting down girls.
3. The girls are drawn by Love Power, and when they touch you, your Love Power decreases.
4. If you run out of Love Power, girls won't come to you, and you'll effectively be knocked out.
5. If you get shot by Izuna, you lose control of your character and become Izuna's "slave of love"—an enemy.

6. Allies whom Izuna has shot to turn to enemies can be brought back by *being shot again by an ally.*
7. The method in #6 can also be used to bring back a player who's run out of Love Power.
8. All character stats *reflect players' abilities in real life*, except that magic cannot be used.

"—So, yeah, is that how it is?"

"Your quick grasp of the rules is a pleasure to see."

...Sora put his hand on his chin and thought. The foreseeable issues and concerns were countless but posed no problem. It was just—really just barely but—within the expected parameters.

"Ah well, it's just a cross between *Le*t 4 Dead* and *Gal*un*, basically."

Tidying up the rules in his head, still Sora had to say.

"But this is really a stupid-ass game...the kind oinking *otaku* buy..."

"...Like...you, you mean."

"Yeah. This stage and protagonist are shit, but it takes some balls to use a game this dumb for a battle for dominion. And I can't really argue with being chased around by animal-girls."

Sora, starting to leer and wheeze, suddenly asked:

"Gramps, this 'Lovey Gun'—if you shoot an ally, they recharge; how's that work?"

"Very simply. It is because it fires Love Power."

"...So it has the same effects as being shot by Izuna?"

"Yes, although only temporarily, the party shot will become a 'slave of—' "

Powww!

Before Ino even finished his sentence, Shiro unremorselessly *pulled the trigger on Sora*. The pink bullet that flew out struck Sora's arm at sonic speed, sending up countless little hearts—

"Oh, my sister—my dear sister! To think all this time, a woman so lovely and adorable was so near me and I didn't realize... Oh, these eyes! I want to tear them from my face!"

"...Hey...Brother, no...we're, siblings..."

Shiro squirmed, flushing, in response to his melodramatic gestures.

"Ah! But what of it? You are right that the world would not condone it, but what indeed has become of *our world*! This is Disboard; this is a game! A world where everything is determined by games—whatever anyone may say, let us go—to a place beyond censorship boards!"

"Hey—*I* have something to say!! Have you forgotten that people are watching?!"

As Steph butted in, not getting what was going on but panicking, further, Jibril broke in.

"Then, if I may speak as well."

Powww. Jibril's point was made with a bullet raining hearts toward Shiro.

"...Jibril...I love you... ♥"

"Aaaaaah, Shirooo! Will you deny the love of your brother?!"

"Ahaaugh! This is an example of a 'love triangle' or '*netorare*,' as described in my masters' literature! I see—even to me, who lacks the emotion of love, there's something about it—!"

"*—Hh!*"

...Sora abruptly came back to his senses.

"Mngh... So you stay conscious even in the 'slave of love' state... It's pretty scary to lose control of your character when you're virtually in the game... I was about to lay hands on Shiro and go beyond the ban..."

Shiro, coming to a little after, glared at Jibril with half-closed eyes, saying:

"...Jib-ril...I'll, punish you...later..."

"Ohh! Forgive me, Lord Shiro! I could not contain my curiosity!"

Having grasped the nuances of the rules, Sora started building a strategy in his brain. The first concern that popped up was—

"Ummm… Steph, we just explained the rules, but did you get it?"

"Heh, I shall not have you underestimating me—*I understood not one whit of it!*"

Da-DUMMM. Steph held her head high, proud, and defiant, leaving Sora to explain.

"Hmm. Okay, then, first, this gun, this is how you hold it."

"Mm, like this?"

"Right, right. And you put your index finger into this hole."

"Yes, yes?"

"Then, try pointing it straight down and gripping with your index finger."

"Like this?"

Steph pointed to the ground as she was told, and pulled the trigger. A *powww* sound. It blasted the pavement—and *ricocheted.*

"…O-ohh…How wonderful you are, Ste-pha-nie—eh-heh-heh, I'll never let you go!"

Steph, now her own slave of love, started hugging herself and squirming around.

"Hmm, so they *do* bounce. This must be the key, Shiro."

"…Mm, I…know…leave it, to me."

Surveying Steph as she squirmed with serious eyes, making arrangements that only had meaning to them, the siblings articulated their strategy.

"'Kay, we'll call this Point Alpha for now. We'll stay in a line until we figure out the game balance. According to the rules, no one but Jibril should have physical stats worth shit. If the girls have Werebeast stats, we might even have trouble losing them. Jibril, you take the rear. Mow down all pursuers."

"*…Yes, sir…*"

"Understood, sir—but is it all right to leave little Dora like this?"

At this, staring at the writhing throes of Steph, Sora said:

"Nah, it's no big deal if Izuna shoots her. She's just Steph."

"You speak truly, my lord. She is but little Dora."

At Sora's decisive dismissal, Jibril abandoned Steph eagerly.

"Now, you *two*, let's go! The fate of the human race depends on this battle!"
"""Yes, sir!!"""

"Eh-heh-heh, how wonderful you are, Ste-pha-nie… Ohhh, why are you so cold?"
Leaving Steph behind as she writhed against her reflection in a pane of glass, the three ran.

■VIEWING FLOOR■

The game had begun. Amid the crowd aghast at the stupidity of the game. A girl, exuding caution, a shadow cast over her dark eyes by a black veil.
—Chlammy was there.
(…Fi, can you see?)
[Yes, reading you nicely, Chlammy; why, I can see through your eyes perrfectly.]
The Elf outside the building—Fi—was synchronizing with Chlammy's vision while conversing with her telepathically. To Chlammy, born in Elven Gard, this was natural, but… (For other races, really, this kind of magic must be unbearable.)

—*Twitch* went Ino's eyelid.
(—Is this…the presence of magic?) Lacking, like Immanity, nerves to connect to spirit circuits, Werebeasts were unable to use magic. However, at the *presence* picked up by his superhuman senses, Ino glanced over.
(…Chlammy Zell! Why is she here…?!) Was she not a spy of Elven Gard sent by Elf into the tournament to decide the monarch—?
(—*So they invited her…*as a monitor from another race.)
—The conditions of the covenant applied only to *the memories of the players and Immanity*. If Chlammy was here reporting to a remote race—Elf—by means of magic, that would mean this whole

game was exposed to Elven Gard. Glaring at Sora as he pranced through the virtual world, Ino thought. (This man—just how far ahead does he prepare...?!)

—Just try and use an obvious cheat. *Then all your shady game tricks are going on display.* That was what was being said by the man's thin smile as he closed his eyes.

[Hee-hee, acting like he doesn't notice... Why, his ears have perked at magic.]

Fi laughed at Ino as he kept looking forward while obviously shifting his attention.

—It appeared that everything was going just as Sora had planned.

(Fi, the game they're playing is *just as Sora anticipated*. A fictitious world, called *cyberspace*, in which magic cannot intervene. It doesn't look like there's anything we can do—)

[Why, I'm quite aware; the important thing is that *we're watchiing.*]

—That was Fi for you. She must have figured it out the day she heard Sora's demand.

(Now the Eastern Union won't be able to pull any *too obvious tricks...*)

The game aside—were the *truth of their trickery* to become known to Elven Gard, whatever Werebeast tried to do from then on...this would be the Eastern Union's downfall. That was why, exploiting a loophole in the covenant, Fi had been assigned as a monitor whose memories wouldn't be erased even if they lost.

(...Well, not to say I'm interested in overlooking any tricks. Fi, help me out.)

[Mmm, well, this rite is very difficult to maintain, you know. But, why, I'll do it for you.]

—Once more looking back at the strategy to beat this game that had been in Sora's memory. No matter how many times she reconsidered it, it was too thin a tightrope, the vital parts all smashed up against each other to form the solution. Yet, just as it was in Sora's memory, it sparkled dazzlingly with the words *certain victory.* What gave him this confidence—what made Sora believe in human potential? Through this game, Chlammy wondered if she herself would be able to touch it.

"...Let's see what you've got—Sora."

Yes, in the eyes of Chlammy, through the veil, was Sora, running across the screen.

■ IN-GAME ■

The team dashing between buildings in the concrete jungle of the fictional Tokyo.

—Sora, deftly dodging the animal-eared NPC girls who swarmed him. His eyes were sharp as he ran through his thoughts. Since the girls were supposed to be Werebeasts, their running speed and other physical stats were extremely high—but. Their movements were such that Sora could somehow manage. Perhaps it was because even Werebeasts had individual variances in physical abilities, and because their movements were predictable, always going straight for the hug. But such things were *not important—the crucial thing* was that there was something funny about these NPCs he'd been taking out with head shots, the habit of a hard-core gamer.

"I think there's a momentary lag—between when the girls disappear and their clothes disappear!"

The eyes of the anal-retentive gamer who wouldn't miss a single frame caught it. You could, after all—*destroy individual parts*! Sora aimed his gun and fired. With a muzzle flash followed by the sound of an explosion, his pink bullet flew, grazing the skirt of one of his pursuers—and while the girl didn't disappear in a flurry of tiny hearts, her skirt scattered into the breeze!

"You actually—you actually can!! This is it! This is the true pleasure of this game!"

—Then could you? No, he would. To take out the part that was as close to the body as could be—namely. The panties alone—it must be possible!!

"Cloth thickness—assuming cotton panties, on average 1.5 millimeters."

Sora, staring at the target, her skirt lost, yet charging at him for a hug at a speed far exceeding the human.

"Allowable impact error under one millimeter...but I can do it—!"

The arms of the NPC coming to embrace Sora swept over his head with the roar of reaped air. Having slightly crouched to let the arms of his assailant pass, Sora let his center of balance fall on as he stepped with his right leg. With the minimum movement required, just two steps, he targeted her rear end. At point-blank range, Sora's muzzle aimed—at striped panties!

"—This is it!"

The shot he fired cut into the panties—and disappeared. However, at the same time, the gal herself scattered pink hearts as she vanished and turned to Love Power...

"Shiiiiiit! What, you can't make them go commando?! God daaaamn it!!"

■ VIEWING FLOOR ■

At Sora's failure to eliminate the panties, the crowd that filled the room. A collective cry of dissatisfaction: *Ohhhhhh......* Forced to bear witness, Chlammy desperately twisted her wrists, trying not to look away.

(It's a tactic, a tactic; there's got to be some meaning behind it; there's something he's trying to find out; hold on, Fi!)

[Why, I'm quite fine...except that your gaze is going all over the place; why, you'll make me sick.]

"Yeahhh, bra destroyed! Cover 'em with your hands; you know how to do it!"

This time, at Sora's words audible from the screen, a cry of glee arose: *Oooooooohhhhh!*

(...Forget this stupid race; let it go where it will...)

Chlammy stopped thinking deeply about it.

[Ah, Chlammy, don't close your eyes; open your eyes, Chlammy!]

■ IN-GAME ■

(—Cool, now time to check the last thing.) Chased by animal-girls, weaving through alleys in deep satisfaction, Sora glanced over. Unhurried, marching along with little steps, yet sticking to Sora like glue, Shiro. Launching herself between buildings, amusedly blowing away the girls behind Sora and Shiro, Jibril. Exchanging looks with the two, he nodded once.

"Shiro, gun performance report."

"…All, approximate…units, meters…"

With this preface, Shiro drew in a deep breath.

"Bullet speed three hundred per second, range about four hundred, no wind or gravity effects, linear, elastic collision, number of rebounds limited only by range, rebound angle proportional to entry angle, simple—"

Completing this lengthy catalog, Shiro sighed, *hff,* and commented.

"…So…tir-ing…"

The sister apparently referring not to the measurement but the speaking, Sora mussed her hair.

"Awww, yeah, good job, that's my Shiro!"

And verifying that her mood had improved a bit, he shifted his attention.

"Jibril, what kind of physical stats do they have for you?"

True to the explanation, Sora's and Shiro's bodies were just as normal. Running made them pant. But what kind of constraints had they put on Jibril?

"To not be able to use magic, after all, makes me feel as if I am not myself. It seems my abilities are set at physical limits. Why, how very inconvenient is a physical body."

What's so inconvenient when she's wall-jumping between buildings… But Sora asked with yet greater caution.

"You mentioned that Werebeast physical abilities *approach physical limits.* So right now you're on even terms?"

"It distresses me deeply to admit this is a reasonable assumption."

However, she went on.

"As I mentioned before, certain Werebeast individuals can use 'bloodbreaks.' If this is incorporated into the game—it may be best to assume that I may even be surpassed for an instant."

—Bloodbreaks… Among the Werebeasts, whose physical abilities approached physical limits, a power possessed by a yet further subgroup, which might even break through physical limits for an instant. This was a game prepared by Werebeast; of course they would incorporate it.

"Man, there's you, and there's Werebeast… The dudes in this world are crazy."

Hff, sighed Sora—but whatever. They'd got their info together.

"So, basically, the enemy intends to seal us off from magic in a virtual space and smack us with what they're best at, combat that showcases the summit of physical abilities—*and they think that'll teach us*?"

Sora involuntarily cracked a chuckle.

—" ", who'd stood at the top of over 280 games in their old world. There was a truth they'd demonstrated to hold for all such games, and it was—

"No matter how complex the game looks, ultimately there are just *two* things you can do."

"Namely?"

To Jibril's query, Sora responded with a wicked smile.

"—*Tactical action* and *coping action*. Basically, it's play or be played."

In other words—the one who seized the initiative would win. It was a truth that applied to all kinds of games. And—

"They don't realize. This is the game humans have been best at since antiquity."

The name of the game—was *hunting*.

"Shiro, you're good, right? *Make sure you keep the running to a minimum*—'kay?"

"...Roger..."
"So, shall we get started?"

——......On the eighth floor of a building several hundred meters from Sora's crew, Izuna hid in a storeroom with just one window. From the window, made opaque to Sora's team by the reflection of the sun, she observed them using her Werebeast vision. The enemy were four, and she was one. However bulletproof the game was, if she dropped the ball, it would be over in an instant. Especially considering the enemy had a Flügel. Izuna figured that before attacking, she'd better analyze the enemy's capabilities thoroughly. Meanwhile, watching the three messing around giddily destroying girls' clothing, she furrowed her brow in displeasure.

—*When's the last time you felt a game was fun?* At Sora's words, Izuna ground her teeth. (Who would ever think this shit is fun, please.) Games were a *struggle.* A means to kill each other indirectly.
...If she lost, many would suffer. For their sake, she had to win at any cost. But if she won, she would debase her fallen opponent and perhaps even take their lives. You called that "fun"? All you could feel was—*guilt* for those who lost. (What's that asshole laughing about, please?) Growing irritated, Izuna's eyes as she glared at Sora sharpened yet further.
—And then she noticed a "bomb" appear in Sora's hand. The hurled bomb flared pink. With a moment's delay, a roar, and *vmm*—the impact from the shock waves.

"—?!"
It shook *the building where Izuna was hiding.* Jumping up like a startled cat, Izuna watched her surroundings closely, her ears pricked.
(...They identified my location, please?! Don't shit with me, please!) After the game started, Izuna had immediately taken her

distance from Team Sora and watched them carefully. Without Werebeast senses—no, even if they did have them, they shouldn't be able to find her. But Izuna's hearing—her ears that picked up everything in a hundred-meter radius like a radar. Did in fact catch footsteps, slowly coming up *this building.* (Those footsteps—are Shiro's, please.) Constant pace, small steps, light weight. The player Izuna had judged the most inconsequential. No—not just Shiro. Sora and Steph, too—the Immanities *hadn't even been a factor in her battle picture.* The reason Izuna hadn't attacked right at the start was just her wariness of Jibril, the Flügel. No matter how much they excelled in games, no matter how much they'd uncovered about the game, it wasn't possible that an Immanity could approach her or sense her approaching—there was just no way their response could be quick enough.

—And yet. What was it about that bomb and these approaching footsteps that gave her the creeps? Suddenly, something felt off. She knew from the sound that this building was crawling with girls. Meanwhile, the footsteps were jogging through them at a *calm, even pace…?*

"—!"

Izuna jerked, flapping her kimono, thrusting her barrel toward the door of the cramped, dust-filled room. The one entrance and exit of the storeroom where Izuna hid. Outside the slightly ajar door ambled a mass of girls. The little light footsteps, heading straight up to the eighth floor and reaching it, then. *Ft*—stopped.

(—?) Izuna raised her ears suspiciously and searched into the situation—and, the next moment. The footsteps went faster all at once. The speed an Immanity child could run shouldn't pose any threat—shouldn't, but—

(—What the hell, please?!) The girls ambling outside—on her floor. Went away, *one for every gunshot,* without exception. A chill ran down her spine. The footsteps, shooting again and again with stark precision, still, without the slightest hesitation or disorder. Without dropping speed, only dropping countless girls, went straight—(Bitch's coming here—please?!)

* * *

There was no longer any doubt about it: her location had been compromised—! How they'd figured it out—at this point, who cared? Working her Werebeast senses to the max, out of the storeroom—toward Shiro, running down the floor beyond her vision. She pulled the trigger. With a bang and a flash, the bullet that flew from the muzzle, with stark precision, threaded through the crack of the slightly askew door, flew into the wall, scattering hearts, and bounced. To pierce Shiro's forehead without fail—Yes, an acrobatic shot using the rebound, even accounting for Shiro's movement, from a spot invisible to her. But—this starkly precise bullet. Whizzed by Shiro's cheek as she *just moved one step to the side* and went past.

(—This is bullshit, please!) Yes, bullshit. To be able to dodge a bullet fired at the subsonic speed of three hundred meters per second. For an Immanity, even if her awareness could keep up, her body—her movement couldn't possibly be fast enough. To say nothing of the fact that we were talking about the physical abilities of an eleven-year-old girl—but. That's talking about *dodging.* Shiro's footsteps, which had so far come running through countless girls without breaking pace. Led Izuna to the *answer.* (Could it be—!) Just to check, she fired another bullet, this time *rebounding twice*, toward Shiro—but.

"...No, use..."

A bullet Shiro had already fired—*intercepted it, after rebounding four times.* (It really—is true, please?!) At this late hour, Izuna's understanding was revised.

—With certainty.

This Immanity—this eleven-year-old girl. Was moving with a total grasp of all objects around her.

—Neither bullets nor NPC girls would suddenly come out of thin air. In the case of a bullet, one would check the position of the target, extend one's arm, line up one's sight, and pull the trigger. In the case of a girl, she would see you, then move, and then try to hug you. They attacked with a series of countless steps—through a process, *deterministically.* Which meant—you didn't have to dodge. All you had to do was *not be there.*

—As a matter of fact, the gamer "　", who had become an urban legend in their old world—in other words, Sora and Shiro—in the FPS genre, crushed with hard-core gamers from around the world. The one who had set the unbeatable records—was not Sora, but Shiro. Her grasp of enemy movements thanks to her diabolical *powers of calculation*, combined with her deductions therefrom regarding their movement patterns and firing opportunities, gave her target-leading and attack-dodging abilities approaching precognition. She truly gave her opponents the illusion that the bullets were dodging her and chasing them.

(—I can't believe this shit, please!!) Of course, Izuna had no way of knowing such stories of Sora and Shiro's old world. What led Izuna to this conclusion was her Werebeast sense—yeah, right. It was her *game sense* that told her—this girl is more dangerous than that Flügel. Panicked, she looked around. She was hiding in a narrow space buried in stock. Facing an opponent who had intercepted Izuna's launched-from-out-of-sight ricochet—*with a ricochet.* This position—was bad.

(—I gotta beat it, please!) To open her escape route, Izuna threw a bomb through the crack in the door.

—But before it could even fly out. A *bullet that penetrated from outside*—exploded it! (Wha—?!)

Booooomm—it went. From the blast roaring through the room, she quickly hid behind the stock and made it through a perilous moment. But the interception—that could only mean it had been known beforehand she would throw the bomb. Shiro's running footsteps, unfazed by even this, finally approached the storeroom, as Izuna's hair stood on end. (Bitch's coming, please!!) Still running, she leaped—and kicked the door. Slicing through the smoke, Shiro flew into the storeroom. But, as a nearby rack crashed as she pulled it down at the same time, Shiro's landing was obscured from Izuna's ears. Listening for breathing—none.

(—No choice but curtain fire, please!) Still under the cover of the stock, she took rough aim and fired madly. Countless bullets flew. Ricocheting, they made the room a force-field hell. But—shortly.

She heard Shiro slowly exhale—and a chill jolted down her spine. Izuna jumped immediately. Kicking off from the floor with crushing force, she smashed through the little window and flew into the air outside the building. Looking back, in the room obscured from vision by bomb smoke, Izuna sensed. *The sound of her entire bullet hell having been intercepted.* And beyond that, the sound of bullets that bounced back and converging upon Izuna's hiding place.

(—W. T. F., please?!) If she'd waited to flee another moment—even one second—the bullets would have rained straight through her body. But Izuna's eyes were opened farther. Not by Shiro who had pulled off this series of events.

—But by something approaching overhead.

"Welll, it's a pleasure to see you. ♥"

(The Flügel—Jibril, please?!) Timed to irrefutably suggest that she'd known Izuna would jump, an *aerial ambush.*

—When did she get on the roof?! Wheezing with astonishment. She might be a Flügel, but in this game, she was bound by physical limits. She couldn't use tricks like magic, and she shouldn't be able to fly, either. But, if she'd walked with her own two feet, there was no way she could have failed to hear—! In consternation, still, Izuna kept her thoughts and senses moving. She caught that a bomb was descending from Jibril's hand.

(—It's for *cover*! Please!) She decided on the spot. Even if she were to intercept the bomb, bullets would assail her from the cover of the explosion. Which meant—never mind the bomb. Shoot Jibril first and take it out second! In a judgment that took an instant literally too instantaneous to be called a moment, she pulled the trigger. But.

"Your aim could use some work."

Though her magic might have been sealed, the physical prowess of a Flügel still was neck and neck with a Werebeast. The bullets were fired in midair at short range, but Jibril *dodged by sight*, twisting her body. The bullets grazed Jibril's belt and scattered hearts as they shredded and vaporized her clothes. The bomb intercepted next exploded with a flash and a boom. Jibril's eyes, lining up her sight to fire a bullet through the smoke—

—Recognized the approach of a *third bullet* and went round. The bullets Izuna had fired—were three. The gunshots heard had been two—but the first had been to lead Jibril in evasive action. The second had been to take the bomb Jibril had thrown for cover *and use it for cover herself.* And the third was the real one—

"So—ah? Oh, right, I can't fly?!"

Jibril, abruptly flapping her wings to dodge, yet her wings freewheeled in vain. Unable to right her posture, she took an inescapable strike to the forehead—

Just before that. Jibril definitely saw it. Izuna, disjointedly—*turning her eyes in panic to a faraway building.*

Suddenly—Izuna twisted her body and took evasive action as profound as was possible. Her hanging sleeve billowed and was pierced by *a bullet from afar*—which destroyed it. A hair's breadth later, a *second bullet* from the same direction stabbed Jibril, who had just been shot by Izuna.

—This fact worked her beastly intuition. A blow that *took back* Jibril immediately after she'd been shot. (What if they *planned* this all, please?!) *Fp*—she lifted her head. To see Shiro, in the window of the building Izuna had burst out of, pointing her gun. But— (This posture is useless for attacking, please!) Just like Jibril just now, Izuna, *forced* to evade by the first shot, had no way of intercepting.

—However fine Werebeast's physical abilities might have been, she couldn't fly. To dodge a bullet in the air with no foothold—to accomplish this absurd feat, she'd "pulled out" her center of gravity. That was all she could do—it was too late to right herself. As she tailspinned down, Shiro's barrel aimed coolly. Counterstrike: impossible. Evasion: impossible. Then—! Detonation. At the bullet rushing on through an inescapable trajectory, Izuna (—!!) grit her teeth loudly and flung up her arm. Her second hanging sleeve that she flapped up in the way of Shiro's bullet was sharply pierced and annihilated. But, at the point of entry, the bullet scattered hearts—and disappeared.

"...That's...you can, *use clothes...as a shield...*"

Never heard anything about that rule, Shiro muttered, impressed. Ignoring the girl, Izuna, using all four limbs, finally touched the ground. In the same motion, she bounded away in a sprint in the manner of a true four-legged animal. And Jibril, who'd been shot in succession, crashed headfirst into the asphalt.

—A moment's silence. But she bounced up as if nothing had happened. With a gaze turned to hearts, Jibril looked afar.

"*Master*... Ahh, my lord...please be by my side! ♥"

Then she charged, smashing the asphalt in her wake. Charged—*the three hundred meters toward the place from which Sora had sniped her.*

—The exchange took place in only eleven seconds from Shiro's original attack.

"*...Hff...hff...*"

In the storeroom, still clouded with smoke, Shiro was terribly out of breath.

—No matter how much like a precision machine she moved, how much she put a computer to shame with her calculations, her body was still that of a mere eleven-year-old Immanity girl, nothing more. All her real stats were reflected in this game as is, including her stamina. And on top of all that, just like her brother, she was a shut-in. Cursed by her eternal lack of exercise—her stamina was *devastatingly weak*. Going limp to speed up her recovery even by a little bit, just waiting there for something, she whispered.

"...I didn't...*hff*...finish...her..."

"It's not your fault. Anyway—"

Responding, three hundred meters away just a minute ago, was Sora. It had been exactly *fifteen seconds* since Sora's bullet had hit Jibril. Jibril, having come to her senses, carried Sora into the storeroom on the eighth floor of the building where Shiro waited.

"Looks like it's fifteen seconds until you regain control...also..."

Descending by Shiro's side, Sora asked.

"...Jibril, did you confirm it?"

"Yes, with these very eyes."

Ffp— Jibril bent by Sora and spoke.

"That she turned in your direction *before you fired*, unmistakably."

Sora answered this report with another question.

"Hmm, I was lying still in wait, and I fired under the sound cover of the bomb's explosion while holding my breath. But she dodged. A shot that took her completely by surprise, a subsonic projectile from a blind spot, during a diversion—"

"Jibril—could you dodge that?"

It was pretty much one of those Zen questions: *Can you detect an unknowable attack?*

"—That would not be possible. Might this be Werebeast's *sixth sense*?"

But Sora smirked at this.

"Don't be ridiculous. If they could do that, that wouldn't be a sixth sense—it would be *precognition*."

The so-called sixth sense was just advanced intuition made possible by the combination of five senses. If they could detect things about which they had no foreknowledge whatsoever, they wouldn't have to lie that they could read minds. They'd be able to hold their own with Elven Gard without playing games like this.

"—In that case..."

"Yeah, no question about it—*cheats*."

Sora scratched his head.

"Man, these are some lame-ass cheats they've got built in here. If we coulda finished her off in one blow while she was treating us like cake, that woulda been sweet—oh, well. All troops to Point Gamma. Jibril, grab Shiro so she can rest. I'll go by a different route."

"Yes, my lord."

■ VIEWING FLOOR ■

"—Wha…"

Ino and Chlammy were dumbstruck at the sight on the screen. The crowd that exceeded one thousand, even forgetting their suspicion of Sora and Shiro, let out a great cheer. It was true they hadn't finished her. But it was clear to see—Team Sora was *owning* the girl of the Eastern Union.

(What…was—that?)

But Chlammy was beyond surprise, doubting the spectacle before her. Taking a game the opponent presented and spinning it as if it were their own. With movements and tactics calculated too deeply to fathom, they'd led their opponent just as they liked.

(Shiro, the one the enemy was worried about the least, *overwhelmed her in a head-on fight*. They forced her into emergency evasion, then used Jibril, the one she'd been most worried about, as a *diversion*, and then, after getting her off-balance in the air without a foothold, sniped—)

[…Wow… Why, it's just incredible…]

Even Fi, sharing Chlammy's vision, interjected as if moved from the heart.

—Yes, tactics so perfect they were scary. But this raised innumerable questions. Though the answers might be somewhere in the countless signs that were in Sora's memory but whose meaning escaped her—

(—How did they identify the enemy's location? How is Shiro so overwhelmingly skilled in combat? And they acted as if everything went according to their plan. How did they grasp—no, *control* the situation so…?)

But more important, most important—

(—How did that Werebeast *evade* that…)

[Just as Sora said, why, that must have been an unknowable attaack.]

Yes, even if she had predicted she might be attacked at that time, to know the position— The words Jibril had spoken to Sora.

(*She reacted before the shot…*did she?)

[—It's a "cheat." A trick—why, they're playing foul.]

(I see, cheating you can't prove… They can just say it's a "sixth sense," and that's that.)

[So, this sort of trick is what *defeated Elven Gard four times…* I see.]

Fi's statement expressed how impressed she was while, with just a twinge of hostility, Chlammy quietly checked out Ino. No expression could be divined from his face—but it had to be the case he was shaken. But still, no sign to indicate that he was playing foul.

(I knew it—they *knew* this game. *More than we do!*) Still expressionless, Ino howled inside. How they could have known it so well? How they could have strategized so far in advance? It shouldn't have been possible for anyone to know the Eastern Union's game better than the Eastern Union—the questions had no end—but.

(…Calm down… Even so, it's no use.) Yes, even so. It wasn't as if they had a chance.

■ IN-GAME ■

"…Still, I must say."

Jibril offered.

"—To corner the enemy with *mathematics…* Quite the novel approach."

Point Gamma—i.e., the park Sora had found with a bad view. The park, surrounded by buildings, closed in by barriers entirely except for the sky and the front, was their new base camp, and Shiro was using its ground as her blackboard, furiously scribbling out equations. She screened through the locations Sora had uncovered where Izuna was likely to hide, applied curves of pursuit and backpropagation to calculate Izuna's location probabilistically, estimated the diffusion using the Dirac delta, and then made generous use of particle filters and linear discriminant functions to further deduce even her expected movements. Jibril's comment was praise from the heart for Shiro's equations and Sora's tactics, which had cornered Izuna. But Sora shook his head with a frown.

"...It isn't some bold trick or anything. *It's necessary.*"

"Could you elaborate?"

"...The reason Izuna didn't come supering at us from the beginning was probably that she was worried about you. If that's the case, then Izuna must be about on your level when we're just talking about basic stats."

Sora inserted with a deep sigh.

"Just for your reference, it takes me about fifteen seconds to go one hundred meters. Shiro will probably run out of breath if you ask her to do it in twenty. So, Jibril, how many seconds would it take you the way you are now to go a hundred meters?"

Lightly kicking at the ground and angling her neck as if thinking, Jibril came out with:

"...*Two steps*, I suppose?"

"Your units are quite odd!"

"Frankly speaking, that's all I can do with this heavy body... Masters, every day you live despite such inconvenience... So stalwart you are... Truly I can only bow my head in admiration."

"...Please don't forget that our stats are still like fifty times lower than yours."

At Sora's sarcastically expectorated words, Jibril looked to the heavens with a tragic mien.

"—W-with such a fragile life, like glasswork, still my masters would challenge me and Werebeast, and even the God! Oh, what courage, what brave souls!"

"Could you shut the hell up, please?"

Sora sighed at Jibril, whose respect was deepening now that she'd glimpsed his and Shiro's powerlessness.

"Well—that's just how outmatched we are in specs. If Shiro had miscalculated a single bullet in that hell, she'd be out. For me, if she even gets close I'm toast—*if we don't use math, it's not even gonna be a fight.*"

Yes, to the crowd, Sora and Shiro must have looked overwhelmingly superior. But in fact—if they so much as let Izuna get near, it would be checkmate for them. Even with Shiro's diabolical shooting, were her aim to wobble from accumulated fatigue, that would be the end.

...In which case, finally there would be no meaningful force left but Jibril.

—Advanced tactics meant that a single error could wipe out everything. To have to rely on an elaborate strategy—looked at the other way, meant that *you had no way other than to rely on it.*

"However, once you just guess what kind of cheat the enemy is using, next time you can formulate a new strategy—and then finish her off, can you not?"

Jibril asked this blithely, but Sora, his a face not relaxed in the slightest, declared:

"No."

"—Pardon?"

In place of Shiro, who was fully engaged in bashing out formulas on the ground, Sora explained.

"The uncertainty principle...ahh, no, I guess I shouldn't go off on things I don't really understand."

Scrabbling at his hair, Sora laid it out in his own way.

"...See, broadly speaking, there are two *ways to win* in a game. Either smash them one-and-done, or keep losing until at the end you flip it all over and run away with the victory. Those are the two."

Sora, explaining while raising fingers, yet shook his head and lowered his fingers.

"But a condition to do the second is that you keep acting like an idiot and get the enemy off guard."

...Yes, just as the previous king did, for example.

"When our opponent knows that we're capable of overcoming her, the second way isn't gonna work anymore. Then our opponent's gonna change her hand to adapt to ours. And then it gets pretty much impossible to make an absolute mathematical prediction..."

Having said this, Sora plopped down by Shiro and sighed.

"Now we're going to have to just *play by the rules.*"

Beside Shiro who bit her nails and bashed out equations, Sora himself, seemed uncomfortable.

"—I'm counting on you, Shiro. Now that we didn't manage to take her with the rush, from here on—we're *winging it.*"

"...Mm!"

—Play by the rules? Against a cheater with deep knowledge of the game and overwhelming physical ability? So basically what he was saying—was that it was more or less a hopeless—

"...Jibril, please help me keep watch. In a game like this that has the concept of stamina, even though Shiro can move like a precision machine, if she gets tired, she won't be able to hold her aim steady—she hasn't got that many shots in her like the ones you saw before. Let's protect her so she can focus on calculating."

To Sora, interrupting Jibril's thoughts with orders, Jibril responded reverently.

"Yes, my lord, it shall be done."

"...Damn, maybe I should exercise a little more on a daily basis..."

With this crack, Sora stood and stared down the oncoming NPC girls boldly, but with a line of sweat running down his brow.

■ VIEWING FLOOR ■

Watching the screen, Ino sharpened his hearing. He could hear the heartbeats of Sora and his friends, sleeping by Izuna on the stage, perfectly. Their pulses told him that Sora's words audible from the screen were not lying. But still the heartbeat of a person whose chance to win had withered away—neither was it this.

—They still had something, muttered Ino subtly at a frequency only Werebeasts could hear, so as not to be detected by the watchful Chlammy.

—Indeed, using the same method by which *he had reported Sora's sniping.*

■ IN-GAME ■

[Izuna, they're at the west park. They've still got an ace up their sleeve. Watch out.]

Yes—this was the Eastern Union's *first cheat.* If they put a blatant cheat in the game itself in a public match and it was revealed, they were done. But on the stage, able to see everything in the game—basically, a *God's-eye view*—could only be detected by those able to hear the frequencies he produced…that is, Werebeast.

"…*Hff, hff…*"

Izuna's ears, hidden in a multiuse building a few hundred meters from Team Sora, picked up Ino's report.

(—Ya don't have to tell me, please.)

There was no way a bunch with strategic skills like that would bet it all on one rush.

(It's still just scouting, but I've got something ready, please.)

How they'd deal with it…would be a *sight.*

[Izuna, are you all right?]

—Izuna, unable to fathom what he was talking about. All right? Of course she was all right. It was true they'd startled her a little, but actually beating her was a whole different—

[…Ah, never mind. I suppose you were just quite startled.]

Look—what are you—

[Your face is tense. Let go.]

——……? Having had it mentioned, she touched her face. He was right; it was tense. But what was this—

(…I'm *smiling,* please?)

—What was that about? What was she smiling about? What was so funny? What was this face?!

(…And, since a while ago—my heart needs to shut up, please!)

How long did it plan to keep beating? She hadn't exercised so much it should be like this. What was she so giddy about? What was she so happy about?!

—When's the last time you felt a game was fun?

(——!!)

As Sora's words flashed through her mind, she pounded the wall. The building shook, and Izuna withdrew her fist from the broken wall and stood up.

(...*Hff*...*hff*...)

[Izuna.]

(Shut up, please!)

This couldn't be fun; she couldn't acknowledge her feeling that this shit was fun.

—She had to finish off those bastards quickly, quickly. She had to get this over with—

——......

"Maaan, I like that they're animal-girls, but it sucks I can't touch them."

Sora, as he spoke, picking off every one of the girls who furiously came to embrace him.

"Why not, Master? You have such a reserve of Love Power, I had assumed that a bit of energy drain would be no impediment to your indulging a bit more your desire to touch them and such."

Jibril, guarding Shiro, chatted non-chalantly with Sora as he just barely dove through a pack of girls.

"That's true, or it would be if they weren't Werebeasts! I mean, if they grab me, I'm not sure I can get them off, and—"

He dodged the hands of a gal flying to hug him. The clutches he'd avoided—crunched into the ground.

"Hey, yo, old fart! In this game, if Shiro or I falls from a building or gets hugged by one of these bitches, aren't we gonna die? What's gonna happen then!"

To Sora's cry, the announcer—Ino's voice—responded.

"Ah, that is not a problem. You cannot die in this game."

"Oh, really? Okay, then, I'll go ahead and—"

"However, please note that the pain will feel as if you are dying."

"Gaaaaaaaaaaaaaaaaaaaaaaaaaaaaaaaaaah, Jibril! H-help me!"

Sora, having allowed himself to be embraced in the hope of some sexual harassment, cried out in agony as bones snapped here and there. Immediately, Jibril took out the girl who had embraced Sora, fretting:

"Master! A-are you all right!"

"*Hff*...*hff*... S-sure...I'm fine..."

Sora sprawled on the ground, enduring the intense pain and even raising a thumb and smiling.

"I did it... I got in a squeeze... Honestly the pain numbed me to all other feeling, but it wasn't bad, yeah..."

"At your iron will, Master—your humble servant can only bow in admiration...!"

—Then. Suddenly, there was a discordant something that wasn't an NPC girl, at which Jibril and Sora swished their guns together. It was—looking at them with eyes devoid of light—

"......Oh, it's just Steph."

With that, Sora unhesitatingly fired eight rounds. Each one hit right on the mark. And Steph's clothes—all of them, except her underwear, were blown away.

"...Jibril."

"Yes."

"You take the handicap."

"Understood."

Solemnly carrying out her lord's orders, Jibril shot through Steph's forehead.

"Ohhhhhhhh, Jibril, not faiiiiiir! Where have you been, going away with everyone and leaving me behind, I'll never let go of you agaiiin! ♥"

"...Maybe we screwed up bringing her along..."

■ VIEWING FLOOR ■

[I-Izuna…]

As Izuna began to watch for the moment for her next attack, Ino's report echoed in her ears.

[Ehh…how do I put it…? It appears *they show no mercy even to their allies.*]

That was all Ino could report. At the unbelievably unbelievable treatment of an ally, both the crowd and Chlammy widened their eyes.

(…That girl, she's too… Must be rough.)

To Chlammy, who'd touched upon Steph's treatment in Sora's memory and felt inclined to sympathize from the heart, Fi remarked:

[Chlammy…I have a feeling you and Stephanie should get along welll.]

—Chlammy decided not to pry into what she meant.

■ IN-GAME ■

…Almost two hours had passed since the start of the game. Team Sora's fourth raid had yet again ended abortively, so back to Point Gamma once more. But this time—

"…So now we're finally stuck on the defensive, jeez."

The muttering Sora, already having lost one of his shirts, watched his surroundings with keen eyes. Was his success in only taking one bullet so far thanks to his prodigious powers of judgment? Or was it the work of the conviction that no one wants to see a man naked? Shiro had already lost her uniform's coat and dress and was down to her shirt, knee-highs, and shoes. Jibril, who didn't wear many articles to begin with, had lost a few of the fasteners on her clothes. Were they to take much more damage, the team would be too exposed.

—By now they were practically an illustration of the word "screwed." As Izuna snuck in from time to time among the NPCs assaulting them, they couldn't help but be on edge.

"...Seems our attacks have stopped working, too... Just a matter of time now?"

"Lord Shiro, what is our next—"

"...Jibril...shut, up...!"

Jibril was likewise showing stress, yet Shiro, pulling at her hair restlessly before the equations that had already spread to fill the ground of the park, bit her nails.

—It wasn't working. No matter how much she calculated, she couldn't find the last thing she needed. Her calculations were perfect, but it wasn't enough to complete the picture— Seeing Shiro's expression, clouded with irritation, Jibril broke a sweat and whispered to Sora.

"...Master...could it be this is futile? Even for Lord Shiro..."

"No, she can do it."

Strongly, with no trace of doubt, Sora, looking around diligently, shot her down.

"In games, *Shiro can do what I can't.* That's the way it's always been, and that's the way it will be."

—With those words. Within Shiro flashed a method to complete the formula. But it was—just too. Faintly, Shiro mumbled.

"...Brother, do you...trust, me?"

"Huh? You think your brother has ever doubted you?"

Slipping past a groupie flying at him and shooting her down in a smooth motion, Sora spoke.

—Yeah, come to think of it. Shiro remembered, in *that Othello game*—the one they'd played with Chlammy. There had been something she still hadn't told Sora.

"...Then, Brother... This, time...*it's your turn*...okay."

"Uh, what?"

Shiro subtly turned up the corners of her mouth. And in the formula that filled the park, with a hand raised vigorously, she smashed down—the last variable.

—*B.* And the next moment—a silhouette flashed across the sunlight for an instant. Between and from the walls of the buildings surrounding the park, Izuna's bullet ricocheted to descend on Sora.

"Oh, shi...! Jibril, follow up—!"

Evasion was impossible. Sora braced for impact, immediately ordering Jibril to shoot him back. But before the onrushing bullet could hit Sora—

"Wha—"

Into the trajectory of the bullet headed to pierce Sora—leaped Shiro.

——......A bullet, obstructed by the sunlight, launched from the air while jumping from building to building. A forced attack. But a shot she could clearly feel bite. Unable to watch it to its mark, Izuna landed on a building roof, fracturing it, and pricked up her ears.

"No, bounce sound—I did it, please?"

To her words which implicitly requested confirmation from Ino—that is, that he check Sora's pulse—without delay, Ino's voice responded.

[Shiro's flatlined...in a completely relaxed state. *No longer in control.* You got her, Izuna.]

——......And, seeing Shiro turn her barrel on Sora with lifeless eyes. Sora, Jibril, the whole crowd watching from beyond the screen everyone shared the same thought.

—Here was an enemy...worse than Izuna. Swiftly getting some distance from Shiro—his instinctual response but one he repressed, Sora stood his ground. Toward the flash of Shiro's muzzle, he *stuck out his wrist,* and his wristband took the bullet.

"Jibril! Above!"

Would Izuna miss a chance like this? It was obviously time to go in again to attack—! Stating his prediction as fact, Sora threw a bomb into the air, and Jibril shot it. The flash of a blast. Toward the shadow she saw for an instant, Jibril fired rapidly while rolling. But she didn't have the luxury of a look. Shiro's muzzle flashing again. But this time Sora stuck out his left foot toward the barrel. In a shower of hearts, his left shoe was ripped apart—and it disappeared with the bullet. (If she shoots—*there's no way I can dodge*! Don't let her fire!!)

—But. Shiro moved her body to the side half a step and lowered her barrel toward the floor.

"Oh, cra—?!"

Grasping what it meant in an instant, Sora howled softly. She'd sidestepped—to attack from a position Sora's *shot-blocking couldn't cover.* Expecting that her bullet, fired at the floor, would bounce three times, or maybe eight times, or maybe more—that it would ricochet surely and accurately, rendering any timing Sora could choose for a counterattack meaningless and drill into him, an inescapable attack, her unswerving conviction drew the blood from his face. Dropping his balance, he took off his remaining shoe on the floor and kicked it. The bullet struck Sora's shoe, scattering hearts, and both disappeared.

—He'd blocked it. But. He'd lost his balance and his shoes. Blocking the second round that would be shot in succession—was beyond his reach.

"Jibriiiil!"

To Sora's summons, Jibril responded on the spot, crossing the distance of ten meters in one step and lifting her master. Then with her second step, she launched them fifty meters all at once. But the bouncing bullet Shiro had unleashed had possibly taken *Jibril's entry and flight* into account. It tore away a bit of one of the metal accessories Jibril wore on her arms.

—The attack based on diabolical calculation, of the kind Izuna must have experienced, gave chills even to Jibril, holder of the finest combat abilities among the Ixseeds. She managed to land and deposit Sora, but Shiro meanwhile had already turned calmly to begin her next assault.

"...We are finished, it seems."

Experiencing it herself for the first time, Shiro's shooting... Now if someone said that was a cheat, Jibril couldn't have argued the point, the Flügel muttered as she trembled. Without Shiro's equations, after all, they had no hope of winning this game.

"...Master. Lord Shiro's decision to shield you escapes my understanding—"

"Yeah—*I understand it*, so don't worry about it."

But Sora's expression as he stared intently at the equations scrawled all over the park...

"The variable *B*—it's *Brother*, i.e., *me*."

...consisted of merely a cold sweat and a strained smile.

"In other words, even accounting for Shiro becoming our enemy, the variable of *me* completes the equation—this magical formula that will take us to the promise of victory...that's what you're saying, right, Shiro?"

As Sora let out a dry cackle at this fact, he found himself targeted by Shiro's barrel once more.

...Shiro's phantom bullet, controlling space to bounce and strike from anywhere, aimed for Sora. There was only one way to avoid it. To read Shiro's attack completely—was what Shiro's attack would anticipate, so he'd have to go beyond that—in short, he'd have to win in a *race to read the optimal solution*. Surely you jest—it's as simple as *impossible*. To challenge Shiro *on her own terms* and win was about as likely as an apple falling up.

"...Jibril, engage Izuna for me."

Sora answered with a gulp. In this situation, even a slight error in judgment would not be tolerated. He had decided he should cut himself off from Jibril, their strongest force.

"...Are you certain?"

"I'll have my hands full with Shiro. If Izuna butts in now, we're screwed. You're the only one who can rival her head-on—buy us as much time as you can."

Of course, this carried the risk of letting Jibril, too, become Izuna's slave—an enemy. If that happened, then everything would really be over. But—

"If that is your wish—"

And Jibril smiled.

"—but you wouldn't have a problem if I went ahead and destroyed that thing...I suppose?"

"...Damn, you learn the wisdom of our world quick, don't you? Of course that would be ideal if you can, but let me say what needs to be said. That's where you die."

"Goodness... Well, let me go and destroy her *normally*, then."

Promptly, Jibril thunked down a step and took off.

Ascending to a tenth-floor wall surface in one step, floating up a hundred meters in the sky with the second. In the same beat, a shot flew keenly toward Jibril's back—but she dodged it.

"You attack as expected—I am grateful that you save me the time of searching."

Catching a glimpse of the enemy—Izuna—at the other end of the trajectory, Jibril sneered. She and Izuna, who lit down upon the roof of a fifteen-story building and readied her gun restlessly, faced each other. Jibril, with a proper curtsy, spoke.

"Good day, *doggy*."

"......"

"My, a sense of déjà vu overcomes me... Could it be that the one I faced when I challenged the Eastern Union and lost—was you?"

Taking Izuna's silence for a yes, Jibril narrowed her eyes.

"I see; I had always been puzzled as to why I would lose to a mere Werebeast, but now I understand."

Jibril. With the smile, indeed, of an angel.

"The conclusion you beasts were able to wring from your intellect was 'Let's invite them into a place where we alone can cheat all we want,' was it? As my master has said that this is a perfectly valid strategy, I have held my tongue, but surely I can say this between you and me."

Her clear and lofty voice—smudged with lethal hostility.

"I suppose it is unreasonable to expect *shame* or *pride* from curs such as you?"

Izuna dropped a bead of sweat and stepped back slightly.

—Rank Six, Flügel. The beings beyond the clouds, whose presence, before the Ten Covenants, would have spelled ruin. Izuna had been startled by those Immanities, Sora and Shiro, but the one she'd been most wary of from the beginning was now in front of her. The instincts remaining in the blood of the Werebeast shrieked. *Drop your weapon. Weep, wail, and beg for your life. What stands before you—is death*, they said. Hushing these instincts with reason, Izuna gripped her gun tighter.

"Well, I have been told by my master to buy time, but we might as well have fun."

Jibril delivered this line with a smile like the sun but with eyes as if she were gazing upon trash.

"Please feel free to expend all the cheats you have and further shame yourself to your satisfaction."

The two launched from the floor, splitting the concrete into the air. Firing with godly speed—their Lovey-Dovey Guns. The two races with the greatest physical power among the Ixseeds, do or die.

—LOVE or LOVED: they cross—!!

—A bullet whizzed by Sora's temple as he ran through the alley. It would be too easygoing to say he dodged it. It was fired by Shiro. Even if he dodged it once, it would only be expected for it to bounce several times and come for him again! Think. What action would his pursuer not be expecting as she aimed through multiple rebounds?! No time, no room for error, but answer in one decisecond!

"Hrrrrg, this is it!!"

With a roar, Sora dared to backstep in the direction from which the bullet came, toward Shiro. Next moment. The bullet that had bounced back sliced past in front of Sora's eyes.

"—Shit, you read everything, even this!"

The only reason he'd managed to escape it was that his decision speed and jump distance had minutely exceeded Shiro's expectation…or something like that. But—next time, an attack correcting for that would come. He knew it: he didn't stand a chance against his sister when it came to reading this kind of thing.

"Aaagh, whaddaya want me to do, Shiro?!"

Thus screaming, Sora kept running. He had so far made it through Shiro's attacks only because of his superior physical capabilities. Shiro had no stamina. So she couldn't run. If she ran, she'd get tired out, and her shooting would lose precision. The advantage of distance and stamina gave Sora the slightest margin in which to think.

(Can't bluff; useless to intimidate; predicts her opponent's actions mechanically and mathematically and blocks them off… If a game came out with an AI like this, the devs would get their asses flamed for making it impossible!) Escaping from the lane of multiuse buildings, he leaped into the next building he saw. What kind of building it was couldn't be answered without asking the Eastern Union, who designed it, but— (Weird entrance, so many curved surfaces—the more curves there are, the harder it's gonna be to—) But his intuition warned him. He ran past and knocked over a nearby table. *Bish*—the bullet hit the table. He'd blocked Shiro's attack, but he felt fear before any kind of relief.

"—?!"

He dropped his posture and leaped, rolling forward. Next moment, a bullet hit a *curved lamp on the ceiling* and landed behind him.

"You can effortlessly calculate ricochet angles off curved surfaces? I know you're good, but, cripes, Shiro!"

He found himself wanting to shout, *You may be my sister, but you've still gotta be kidding me!*

"Shit, it's hopeless. This is beyond fixing with a different playing field…"

—Run. Fast, but with small steps, irregularly! Rule out the expected patterns and then rule out the patterns that would be expected then and then rule out again! Make it to the roof! If you get to the roof, you can narrow down somewhat the places the bullets can—

(—And she's gotta be expecting that, too. If she's operating continuously in an uncontrolled state using the optimal solution—)

In Sora's heart, where feelings of despair now wandered—a question popped up. (Wait, isn't it weird…?) So far, Shiro had *never run*. When Sora had threatened to escape her range, she had closed the distance by blocking his exit. She'd gone on with her precise shooting, without using up her stamina, without tiring, but—

(…If she was really trying to do me in, there must have been a time she coulda got me if she ran…) The one who'd ordered Shiro not to run—was *him*, wasn't it? Because she'd need to save her shooting precision to face off with Izuna. But if her goal was simply to finish him, what difference would it make if she ran out of breath a little? If it were Jibril, then all the more, so—

(…If I'm wrong about this, that's gonna smart…but hey.) Sora decided: no choice but to do it.

He kicked down the door and got on the roof.

"*Hff, hff*… Sooo, Shiro? Your brother's about at his limit. How can you treat a shut-in like this…*hff*…?"

Tailing him, Shiro showed up on the roof. In her eyes, still—no light resided. Walking, swaying, she gently aimed her muzzle toward Sora. (Tenth story above ground. No tall buildings nearby—)

"Uhh, Shiro… If I'm wrong about this—"

Sorry, he was about to say, but he changed his mind. He couldn't afford to be wrong about this. He wasn't wrong. This was the right answer. When they'd played Chlammy, he'd left Shiro to take care of a follow-up of that magnitude. This was no time or place for her *big brother*—to fail!

"——Rrrraaaaaaaaaaaaaaaaaaaaaaaaaaaah!!"

He kicked the concrete floor and dashed. Shiro's finger pulled the trigger. He swung out the long sleeve of his remaining shirt. She was unmistakably aiming at his forehead—he put his sleeve in its trajectory. Impact. His last shirt flew away, exchanged for hearts and bullets. But blocking the bullet to his forehead had shut off his vision for a moment. What he should do in that time was clear. Several shots rang out. He couldn't see. But conviction told him. Shiro was aiming to ricochet them off the sides and the entrance to the roof to create a *horizontal bullet hell force field*...! If there was a zone of safety—it could only be the result of an action Shiro wouldn't expect. If there was something that wouldn't occur to Shiro, it was:

"—*Not trying to dodge at all*, yeah?"

With that. Sora flew straight toward Shiro's body. Momentarily, Shiro's eyes bugged out. He went on to embrace Shiro and fly over the fence and off the roof while countless bullets whizzed by his back. And while falling, Sora stuck his gun toward Shiro.

"—Don't worry. They say you don't die when you fall. I'll be on the bottom for you."

Point-blank range. Pulling the trigger, Sora grinned. The shot rang through the cluster of buildings—and landed.

"...Brother...I love you. ♥"

Squeeze! Shiro hugged Sora, who reciprocated.

"Yeah, your brother loves you, too."

[*Izuna, now.*]

—In response to the whisper in her ear. Izuna crashed through a window and sailed out from a building across the street. Her gaze and muzzle fixed on the falling Sora and Shiro. It was a reenactment of the scene that had been imposed on Izuna in the first raid. Sora, holding a non-player-controlled Shiro, in free fall from the roof of a ten-story building. Unable to reorient. Unable to—escape.

(—You bastards have given me enough trouble, please.)

But Sora, not even looking at Izuna as she came to greet them.

"...Ha-ha, seriously, it's just pathetic."

Smiling with pleasure from the bottom of his heart, in his hand—a bomb.

"—?!"

The haphazardly released bomb was shot down reflexively by

Izuna—who in an instant regretted it. (No—I screwed up, please!) The flash that came immediately burned Izuna's retinas. At the boom that assaulted subsequently, her eardrums went numb. Her hearing was sealed off. In her flickering vision, bullets cut through smoke and flew, and she just barely dodged them—by dumb luck, Izuna admitted, awestruck. (He figured it out, the bastard...no, that's not it, please.) How he'd seen her attack coming was of no interest. The real question was— (How'd the bastard shoot with such damn precision, please!) Holding a non-player-controlled Shiro, unable to see, and yet shooting precisely from midair. Sora may have been one hell of a gamer, but how could an Immanity possibly— But Izuna's thought was force-stopped. Her senses, still unsteady from the bomb blast, even so detected it surely. In the falling Sora's arms. Shiro, supposedly non-player-controlled, calmly, mechanically, and accurately—pointed at Izuna. Shiro's eyes, *clearly paragons of sanity, fixed straight this way—*

"That's why—*you saved your energy instead of running*, right, Shiro?"

"...Brother...I love you."

Shiro with a grin. The same line as before, but drily this time.

■ VIEWING FLOOR ■

"Impossible—?!"

At this spectacle, at last, Ino cried out. Ino had been relaying the exchanges of Sora and his friends to Izuna the whole time. He thought he'd given the timing and instructions for raids perfectly. And of course, he'd been listening all along to the heartbeats of the fleeing Sora and the pursuing Shiro. The rule was that being shot by the Lovey-Dovey Gun would rob one of control for fifteen seconds. But it hadn't even been two seconds since Shiro had been shot by Sora. Sora's shot had definitely hit Shiro. He'd even heard it. But then...how?! Then—at that moment, Ino and Izuna both hit upon the same possibility at the same time.

■ IN-GAME ■

(The bastard faked it by having it hit her clothes, please?!) Shiro, falling in Sora's arms. If they had faked the impact, she should have some article of clothing missing—but it didn't look like... But then, in a blink, she felt something off about the clothes billowing in descent. The line from Shiro's hip to her leg penetrated into Izuna's eyes. And she remembered the shit Sora was pulling early—(No way—really—) On the eve of this decisive showdown on which Immanity's fate depended.

(—The bastard really just went for the panties, please?!)

It was an absurd conclusion—but, still, that wasn't enough to explain the situation. If the shot Sora'd just fired was a sham, Shiro should still be Izuna's slave. But the fact that Shiro was sane and pointing her gun at her led to—just one conclusion. As if jeering at Izuna's thoughts, Sora spoke.

"You finally get it? From the beginning—*Shiro's never been on your goddamn side.*"

The shot when she'd shielded Sora—truly, it was a fine performance; it had even deceived Sora. Looking down at Shiro's dress shirt, flapping in the wind, there was one... Spot the difference: *Just one button* was missing. Back then, Shiro had blocked Izuna's attack at the cost of *just one button*. Only Shiro, who could read the trajectory of a bullet in units of millimeters—could pull off such a divine performance.

■ VIEWING FLOOR ■

(That—that can't be!) Unconvinced by this fact, Ino screamed inside. (Sora was sincerely panicked! And Shiro's heartbeat had none of the tension of plotting something!) Shiro's pulse, since being shot by

Izuna—and even now. She was relaxed body and soul. Her heartbeat pulsed as flat as could be. But then that would mean—

(She *deceived even her brother*?!) That she'd deceived her brother, without tension, or worry, or excitement—without a trace of unease. With no prior arrangement, entirely ad-lib, they'd coordinated...!

■ IN-GAME ■

—But Izuna, in the field, didn't even care about that, either. No matter what kind of trick they had pulled, this situation could only mean one thing. (*The bastards got me*—please.) It meant that a painstaking web of intrigue had caught her once more. Having lost her balance dodging the initial barrage—the one she aimed for was that "Shiro." There was no way she could miss, and the clothes that once served as a shield remained hardly at all.

(But—*that's all*, please.) The window of the building Izuna had crashed out of—beyond it. From the darkness, a figure brandishing a firearm was lit by a muzzle flash. The one whom Izuna'd defeated—the turned Jibril. The bullet released sprinted keenly through the sky to attack Sora and Shiro. (Looks like they laid a hell of a trap—but this is the end, please.) Izuna was one step above them. That was all, and now it would end— As Izuna thus assured herself of her victory, her body—

—now convulsed with a violent, irresistible throb that enveloped her. Shiro pulled the trigger, and light spewed from her muzzle. At the same time, Izuna realized—the child *wasn't aiming for her*. She felt all the skin on her body crawl. It was...Werebeast's unmistakable—"*sixth sense*." Shiro's muzzle and her eyes both had been fixed from the start *beyond her*. At *Jibril*.

—But, having grasped that, who could anticipate? That, as Jibril fired her own bullet—

* * *

—Shiro's bullet was aimed to ricochet off it at Izuna—what a ridiculous idea.

Outguessing and plotting, layered thick and knotty. The counter to the counter to the counter to the counter was impossible to predict—no, even to imagine. The bullet landed at Izuna's rear—and bounced. To attack Izuna from her blind spot. A fatal blow impossible to respond to or even see coming. The attack Shiro had launched, deceiving her brother, deceiving Ino, deceiving Izuna, and even incorporating Jibril's defeat. With such godly—no, *diabolical calculation*, there was no way it could be dodged. No, definitely no way.

—Under normal circumstances.

"*—Now it's getting fun*, **please!!**"

Crowing. Izuna bared her teeth and sneered. At the same time, blood pumped out of control throughout her body. Her capillaries bursting, her eyes and fur were stained scarlet with blood. Her nerves heated up, her cells boiled, her muscles erupted, the laws of physics roared.

Bloodbreak. The crimson form said to shatter the limits of physics—

Izuna's arms, wet with blood—disappeared without a sound. It was beyond the abilities of the two Immanities, Sora and Shiro, to even comprehend. Izuna's arms, swung down at a speed no one could perceive—*grasped the air*. Her hands, outrunning sound, generated enough friction against the concentrated air to catch her falling body for a moment. And with a subsequent "kick," she leaped. While Izuna subjugated inertia and gravity with brutal force, below her the instant-kill bullet—slid...past.

—What kind of nonsense was this? The impossibility of this feat, which defied everyone's comprehension. But to those who were intimately familiar with games, the phenomenon could be explained in a single phrase. Izuna's muzzle tracking from a new position, her beastly eyes awash in crimson. Feeling them aimed directly at his forehead, Sora could only—chuckle.

"—A *double jump*? Give me a friggin' break, ya big cheater."

Here it was, that "bloodbreak" thing Jibril had described. Among Werebeasts, who approached physical limits, one who could transcend them.

A single gunshot was heard. But two bullets fired within the same instant bolted toward the falling pair. With nothing to obstruct their paths—the phantom bullets penetrated the foreheads of their targets almost simultaneously. Sora and Shiro, unmoving and helpless, crashed to the ground like broken toys cast away. Next, Izuna landed in the posture of a four-legged animal, and the asphalt cracked gigantically.

"Hhhhhhhhhhhhh...Hhhhhhhhhhhhh..."

The look of a beast, an embodiment of violence, breath fierce, raring for combat. Her bloodstained sublimity gradually blackening in the air—

■ VIEWING FLOOR ■

"...—"

Silence. The crowd watching through the screen was soundless. Even Chlammy, even Fi, who must have been watching the same scene, had no words.

—This was Ixseed Rank Fourteen, Werebeast. Now, at last, Chlammy realized. So late she had no excuse, but— Why the Eastern Union had accepted this game. Why they had answered the call for a public match which would disable almost all cheats. It was true that Sora had laid countless traps. But there had to have been other ways to go about it. But the Eastern Union had taken up this game anyway for this plain and simple reason. No matter what kind of calculation or strategy they faced—all they had to do was sweep it aside with the ludicrous absurdity that was their overwhelming difference in power. Though only two ranks above Immanity—monsters too overpowered to comprehend. With this before her, Chlammy herself gulped and despaired.

—There was no way they could win. Fi's silence and Jibril's defeat said everything. To beat these monsters in an arena from which magic was sealed off, was probably beyond the abilities—of any of the Ixseeds. Izuna herself—Werebeast itself, in this zone, was the *worst cheat possible*. (So this…is what the Eastern Union's game is really all about?) An impossible game that defied reason. This was the truth behind the Eastern Union's game.

Ino, his head cool, momentary shock subsiding. Diligently checking Sora's and Shiro's heartbeats.

—Both siblings, flatlined. Perfect head shots, impossible to fake. But at Izuna's heartbeat beside them… At that explosive sound, beating as if to leap out of her body to echo through the hall…

[You finished them, Izuna; it's done; calm your blood!]

Ino called to Izuna in a cold sweat.

■ IN-GAME ■

"—Hhh!—Hhh!—Hhhhhhhhhh…"

Ino's voice didn't make it into Izuna's ears. But she didn't need the report; she knew she'd definitely finished them. It wasn't the bodies of the two, sprawled limp on the ground, but her intuition that decreed she'd gotten them. Izuna, who had taken action that bent the limits of Werebeast, wrestled down the very laws of physics. Her heart, spinning to make it possible, slowly revved down. As if just now remembering the laws of physics, agony assailed every inch of her.

—Her body was terribly heavy. Though she struggled to steady her breath, it wouldn't settle. Her muscles were shredded, her blood vessels had burst, her nerves had melted— For Izuna, literally broken, even standing had become heavy labor. But it didn't matter. It had been worth it. She had had to. Now—

"...I win, please..."

Muttering painfully, Izuna stood up on two legs. Dropping her gaze to Sora and Shiro, sprawled and still, she opened her mouth to say something,

———and, *poof.*

All too unceremoniously. All too suddenly—Izuna's arm...was struck by a bullet.

"...Huh?"

...Forget Izuna. Everyone watching...even Ino, even Chlammy, even Fi. All uttered a dumbfounded noise and turned their attention to where Izuna was gaping—the direction from which she had just been hit. And they saw...

...clinging to the back of an NPC girl, eyes closed, arm, hand, gun extended—

"So-Sora, is that all right? May I open my eyes now?"

Steph. Yes, Izuna had indeed used her "sixth sense" to dodge an attack impossible to dodge. But—that still *wasn't enough.* As Sora had said, the ability to know things of which *she had no foreknowledge* was not one possessed. To achieve that kind of cheating would require magic or superpowers.

What Shiro had been furiously calculating on the ground of the park—was the strategy to take down Izuna *by no means.* It was—the *wander algorithm* of the NPCs' meandering, but there had been no way to know that. That in reality—*it had all been one formula,* just to deduce how to lead the girls, while affecting them, as they ambled in search of Love Power. All the tactics Immanity's team had deployed—from the first volley to their cornering. All had just

been tactics that Shiro had calculated out, preparing countless scenarios before the game. Everything that had transpired during their match had done so according to Shiro's design.

It had all been a formula purely to build this one moment.

"...However much you might have some 'sixth sense'..."

In Izuna's vision, display of the word *DEFEAT* signalled the end of the game. Everything over, Sora and Shiro stood and spoke.

"The one Shiro was aiming for when she bounced that bullet off Jibril's *wasn't even you—*"

"...Be-low..."

"It was someone getting carried here on the back of an NPC girl with her eyes closed—you'd never guess it was Steph, would you?"

At these words, Izuna's eyes widened. The bullet that had been made to rebound outside her line of sight to attack her—was *Jibril's.* It had ricocheted outside her vision not to mount an inescapable attack—but so that the bullet's *target would not be*...obvious?

Before the game, Steph had had a "very special charm" performed on her by Sora. Namely—

"Obey the command Shiro writes on the ground. But forget about it—that was the covenant I bound her with."

Sora smirked wryly.

"A formula to enable a roving Steph, drained of energy, mounted on the back of an NPC girl, whose only instruction was 'Shoot ten seconds after you get a Love Power boost,' to aim for Izuna and fire...it's no wonder Shiro was struggling."

Feigning she'd turned to Izuna's side and leading Sora. And then Sora *feigning that he'd shot Shiro back.* Izuna then attacking while getting cover fire from Jibril. An attack predicting and using all this being dodged—and being shot: Their strategy accounted for all of this.

"No footsteps 'cause she's riding piggyback. No sense of hostility 'cause she doesn't remember. No consciousness, even, 'cause she's already inoperable, but thanks to the Covenants, *actions can still be executed.* Steph, who'd gone off everyone's radar since the beginning of the game—firing the one moment when Izuna had used up all her power…"

If you could see that coming, let's see it, Sora implied emphatically as he smiled.

"—This is one thing that, even with a 'sixth sense,' would be *unknowable*, right?"

Ino stared at the screen, his thoughts resounding as if howling in his mind.

(Impossible! That's not even on the level of "calculation"! That's—)

But Sora pulled up his lips as if to sneer at the Werebeast's inner monologue.

"'That's goddamn precognition'—ain't that what you're thinking, *Gramps*?"

(Wha—?!)

Sora grinning ear to ear, and Shiro smirking likewise.

"The whooole time, you were monitoring our heartbeats and reporting to Izuna, right?"

—They'd caught it: No. It wasn't even something so half-assed as that. Yes, this explained everything.

"*…I see, so you* exploited it…"

Ino's understanding getting there: In other words, just as Sora had said—

"That's right—in a game, ultimately there are just two things you can do."

Namely, tactical action and coping action. All kinds of games, when you got down to it, were just a matter of wresting away the initiative.

"The initiative was in our hands the whole time. That's all there is to it. You thought you were playing, but you were just *being played*—the result is fate, not precognition.

"By the way, Shiro."

"…Mm."

"What was that variable *B* you subbed in anyway? If you were conscious from the beginning to the end, then you saw the endgame in its entirety, didn't you?"

"……So, they…wouldn't, catch on…"

When her heartbeat was being monitored, though she might fake taking a bullet, she couldn't cover up her psyche. Therefore—Shiro had to maintain a relaxed state while giving all she'd got. One whom she could know she couldn't beat even fighting for real. One whom she could trust to see through to her intent.

"…I, couldn't think…"

A variable that could fulfill these parameters. Since that day at the end of her infancy and up to the present. As far she knew, only one "magic number" so convenient existed.

"…of, anyone…but, you…"

Shiro could always do what Sora couldn't. And so—naturally, the converse also applied. Thus, Sora said with a wry smile.

"Yeah, we don't have any obligation to bother with *combat.*

"The weak have their own way of doing things. We'll leave fighting lions with one's bare hands to the *lions.*"

■■■

As the audience erupted in cheers, all of the game's players were coming to on stage. The siblings were holding hands tightly, and Shiro spoke as soon as their eyes opened.

"…Anyway, Brother."

"Mm? What is it, my sister?"

Sora responded as if reluctant to release her hand.

—Inwardly, he'd realized that being forced to operate separately from Shiro—even in a virtual reality—had given him chills.

"…Why'd you, go to the trouble of, leaving my shirt…and, shooting…my panties…?"

"Wha?! Don't ask something so obvious, okay, Sister?! You think I could let this huge crowd see you naked?!"

"You speak as if I didn't matter!"

Having awoken a step behind, today's MVP—Steph—howled.

"Now, now, little Dora. No one can deny that your fine play made the day. Would you care to comment on how it feels to have been entrusted with such a decisive moment for the fate of Elkia?"

"May I answer honestly? I have no interest in going through this again!!"

The pressure of having been responsible for the fate of Immanity. If Sora hadn't been so kind as to *erase her memory*, there was no way in blazes she would have accepted it, she screamed. Meanwhile at her side, rising together, Sora and Shiro.

"So, we still waiting for the victory announcement, Gramps?"

Sora prodded Ino.

"—Winner: Elkia... By the law of the Covenants, the Eastern Union shall transfer to the Kingdom of Elkia all its rights on the continent of Lucia..."

At Ino's declaration, delivered as if chewing sand, the acclamation of the crowd rose to greater heights.

—Who could complain about a king and queen who had taken down Werebeasts and doubled their domain with a single move? Yet despite the crowd's unbridled enthusiam, what came next was enough to inspire a hush.

"Likewise, by the law of the Covenants...Izuna Hatsuse...and I, Ino Hatsuse, both surrender all our rights—to these two, the monarch of Elkia..."

"Yes, very good."

As Sora nodded decisively, Steph and the audience stared bug-eyed. Yes—their demand had been for *all the Eastern Union had on the continent*. That included all the resources and territory—as well as all the people and technology.

"So now we pick up a scad of Eastern Union technology and get Izzy and all the Werebeasts on the continent all in one fell swoop—huhhh. Man, oh man...it was worth the effort we put in."

Steph shivered at her master's happy-go-lucky tone as he stretched. What Sora had said the other day, "We'll conquer the world. All of it—whabam—no two ways about it." She'd touched upon his meaning—but at the same time, Steph caught sight of Izuna from the corner of her eye.

"......"

Face downcast, motionless. Ino, wringing out carefully chosen words but nevertheless doing what he could, attempted to console her.

"Izuna… You bear no responsibility… It was a decree of our homeland, which I ordered…"

—Having come this far, Steph finally understood what Sora had meant. What rested on those little (all too little) shoulders which shook as Izuna stared down…

—The burden, all too massive, of the entirety of the Eastern Union's rights on the continent. Having lost these, how many…of Izuna's brethren would lose their homes, their jobs, be cast into the streets—perhaps even lose their lives? Steph recalled her own accusation.

—"How do you intend to take responsibility?!"

—There was no way to take responsibility.

The agent plenipotentiary was entrusted with the lives of hundreds of thousands. One capable of bearing all the responsibility thrust upon this position could not exist. The one who'd made light of the title…was not Sora, but rather… (It was…me, I suppose.) Steph hung her head, but Sora carried on unaffected.

"It's not like that, right, Izuna?"

"Uh?"

"—It's that it was so fun, *you don't even know what to do with yourself,* right?"

Ino and Steph gasped. At the very end, when Izuna had unleashed her bloodbreak… She had—clearly—said as much.

—Her exact words: *"Now it's getting fun."*

"…That's, bullshit, please…"

But.

"Now that I've lost, a bunch of assholes are gonna suffer, please."

Izuna couldn't admit it.

"But—why is it, please?"

She mustn't admit it—and yet…

"Why—why'd my goddamn face smile, please?!"

Izuna's mind flashed back to their final encounter in the air. The moment she'd clearly felt, *this is fun*.

"Could I perhaps have won if I hadn't been distracted by that bullshit then, please?! Now people are gonna die because of me, please?! 'Cause I—thought it was fun!!"

"I-Izuna, calm down—you—"

Izuna's indiscriminate wailing—she knew no other response—silenced the floor. Ino, too, was at a loss, just holding her shoulders, trying to soothe her. But still there was Sora.

"Relax, Izuna."

Approaching the frenzied Werebeast, Sora gently parted his lips.

"No matter what you'd done differently, we'd already beaten you anyway."

Somehow uttering this yet beaming like daylight, Sora froze the entire assemblage. *Is that the best this man can offer by way of comfort?!*—thought Steph, aghast. Next to the trembling Izuna, though, Sora knelt, stroking her head.

"Besides, it seems like you're confused—*no one's gonna die, and no one's gonna suffer.*"

"…Huh?"

"*This world is a game.* You've got it wrong fundamentally, all of you."

These words—the same that Sora had mumbled in the past both to Steph and to Jibril. But to this day, their true meaning remained obscure.

"Looks like you're not convinced. Then let's do this."
And then Sora made an interestingly timed proposal.

"No tricks. No cheats. You and me, let's duel."
So he proposed, with a mischievous smile like that of a child.
"If I win, I'll tell you how I know. If I lose—let's be friends, okay?"

■■■

Displayed across the screen for the crowd's viewing pleasure was the center of a street along which buildings were aligned. The audience watched in fascination as, not unlike in a Western, the breeze blew scraps of paper across the scene. The shadows of the opponents squaring off. Sora, king of Immanity. And Izuna, representative of the Eastern Union.

Shiro, Steph, and Ino gazed intently at their images on the screen. Chlammy squinted hard at the display while Fi shared her vision. And—just as during the epic battle on which Immanity's fate itself had been staked, the thousand-strong crowd peered transfixed at this match, which was nothing more than a silly wager.

The game Sora had proposed was simple. Sora and Izuna would face off head-on, using their real physical abilities.

—There was no way he could win. Such was the opinion of all who had seen that vermillion visage of Izuna. It was true that Team Sora had managed to conquer even that. But by no means had it been head-on. They'd just barely taken her down using wiles, tactics, and traps upon traps laid thick and countless. An Immanity, in terms of pure reflex and speed of movement, didn't stand a chance against that scarlet devil. Now that all the Eastern Union possessed on the continent had been seized, Izuna and Ino, of course, were included in that. Sora's possession of Izuna was a done deal. So this challenge could only be interpreted as some pedantic way of implicitly consoling her, "Let's be friends." But at the same time, everyone there wondered. Had this man, the king, one half of Immanity's greatest gamer—*this fraud*—ever done anything just as he said?

"'Kay, ready? I'm gonna toss this coin, and it'll be a battle to see who's the quickest draw from the moment the coin hits the ground."

"...—"

Sora took Izuna's silence as acceptance. With a ting, the coin floated high in the air. In Izuna's dark eyes, betraying no emotion, Sora's face was reflected.

—The only one who had defeated her. The one who had taken all the Eastern Union's continental territory in a single move and cornered countless Werebeasts. The one who had dismissed all of that with "*No one's gonna die*" and dangled the promise of proof before her.

—The coin made a sound as it struck the ground. But...Izuna just cast her eyes down, making no move to draw.

"Hm... Well, I guess you would choose that."

With that, Sora laxly drew his gun and pointed it toward Izuna.

...Yes, if Izuna lost intentionally, Sora would show her the proof that no one would die. If it was reasonable, Izuna would be relieved the weight of responsibility she carried. Even if it made no sense, she'd be under no obligation to befriend the bastard who'd bested her. However you looked at it, the scenario was designed so Izuna would lose intentionally.

—That was fine. All she had to do was allow herself to lose and then ask him for his damn reassurances. And then—and then—

"...Hmm, can I tell you honestly?"

Sora sighed. In a deep hue of disillusionment, Sora tightened his index finger, pulling the trigger.

"I'm disappointed in you, Izuna."

———!

"—Don't screw with me, please!"

Then Sora's muzzle flashed and bullet fired. Izuna lifted her face *eyes stained scarlet.*

—Bloodbreak. The crimson beast's movements, faster than the speed of a bullet. Her gun drawn at a speed impossible for an Immanity's eye—for Sora's eye—to follow. Powerful enough to shatter the shackles of physics. A draw worthy of being called divine. Though launched after Sora's, Izuna's projectile collided with Sora's near the *midpoint between the two*, altering the trajectory of each. Izuna's second round instantaneous. Dead on target—Sora's forehead. The deed done—the trigger pulled—she wondered:

(—What am I, doing, please?) Why was she trying to win? This was when she should be asking Sora—for the sake of Werebeast, for the sake of the Eastern Union—how he knew no one would die. And yet...how come—

Irrespective of Izuna's inner turmoil, her bullet barreled on. And as Sora tipped his head to the side slightly...it brushed harmlessly past.

"——Huh?"

As if— No. Definitely, *just as he'd predicted*. But by then...already. Sora's *second round*. Even to Izuna's Werebeast eyes—with the benefit of her *bloodbreak*—the bullet was so close to her chest that just noticing was the limit.

—A shot made in the knowledge that Izuna would fire a second round. Timed to Izuna's muzzle flash. In other words, discharged in the fraction of a second during which the Werebeast's senses were obscured. As Izuna felt the bullet sink into her chest, she was sure she heard Sora's voice in her ears.

"Yeah, *that's what I'm talking about...* That's the real you."

Izuna's vision as she fell was filled with a canopy that stretched out endlessly.

"I'm sure you do care for the other Werebeasts who'd suffer when the Eastern Union loses. But there's a deeper reason, way down at your core, why you've been crying, and it's simple."

As Izuna drifted, unable to comprehend that she'd been bested, Sora continued.

* * *

"—*You were sad to have lost for the first time*, right?"

——……

"If you're not sad when you lose, you fail as a gamer. But—

"—that's exactly why *it was finally fun.*

"A game you go into knowing you'll definitely win is just work. There's no way you can find value in that, and when people's lives are at stake over something so meaningless, it's only natural you'd even feel like it's a pain in the ass—you've been right all along."

But—

"…How does it feel? Knowing there's someone you can test your whole mind, body, and spirit against and still not beat."

An image of the little girl he'd met long ago flashed through Sora's mind.

"To think about how you're gonna take on this hopelessly OP opponent and bring them down, how you're gonna win, what you're gonna do to defeat them."

The white-haired, red-eyed girl who held within her humanity's potential, which defied imagination. As if recalling his shock at that time, Sora concluded with a heated smile.

"To put it mildly—*sky-high*, right?"

—That might be so. That might be the identity of the impulse that had prodded Izuna. He was the one who had beaten her, and that was the very reason…she didn't want to let him screw with her. She wanted to win next time. That was the very impulse…surely…

"If you understand that, we're already friends. Welcome, Izuna, to *our* side."

Surely, for Izuna, this was the first game she'd played in her life, she thought.

"So, lemme tell you that reason like I promised. Lend me that cute ear of yours."

What Sora whispered into Izuna's flattened ear as he knelt, he did so with the manner of a child plotting some mischievous prank. But a prank that, once imagined, made you start getting excited, too. But at the same time, a caper so dubious in its sanity, so improbably grand in its scale—that it sounded like fun. Having heard the reason, Izuna, as if finally relieved, as if satisfied, closed her eyes with a sense of rejuvenation, saying with a smile.

"Next time... You're goin' down, please..."

At the scene playing out on the screen, the floor was enveloped in silence. Not a peep emerging from the crowd, Steph alone muttered:

"How improbable..."

To win against an opponent so vastly superior in response speed, physical ability, and even senses in a one-on-one battle of wits. Reading Izuna's personality, predicting she'd go for the head shot. Reading the hatred of defeat bottled up under all the responsibility and pressure like magma. Predicting that, after intercepting a bullet, she'd send in a second. And in response, the moment she fired—shooting his own second round...an inescapable bullet. It was proof of what Sora had declared in a speech before.

Chlammy chewed over the words she'd assimilated from Sora's memory.

"—Immanity, through learning and experience, gets *wisdom* approaching precognition, does it?"

Murmuring this, she turned and walked off the floor.

[Oh goodness, Chlammy. Why, are you leaving already?]

(I've already seen everything necessary. The rest—is their job.)

—Don't believe in humans, but believe in their potential...how amusing.

"Very well. I suppose I may as well give it a chance."

Casting off her black veil, Chlammy smiled with her face exposed.

"Fi, *after you get your memory altered for us by Sora*, we're going straight back home. There's much to do."

Cameras okay, memory check okay, steam okay.

"...Confirmed. Sufficient steam to judge wholesome, confirmed... okay!"

And another day with Sora turning his back and welcoming.

"Verrra well, m'dears, don't stand on ceremony; come on in."

"...Why do I have to take a damn bath, please?"

"For my master has determined that it shall be a ceremony to achieve understanding when we welcome new comrades. When my master says, *let there be light*, there is light. It shall be carried out in the name of honor."

"Anyway, Shiro, you seem in good humor today. Did you overcome your hatred of baths?"

"...I'm, excited...to, wash...Izzy's...tail."

Though noise abounded, no figures were seen— Nay, none could be seen. But through the self-restraint he'd tempered like steel, already the very desire to turn was gone from Sora. Owing to his success upon Chlammy and Fiel's visit of capturing everything on video perfectly!

"Heh, everything from the camera angles to the potential for lens clouding, from everyone's entrance to where they'll stand and sit— I've figured out everything using a tablet app, and though I can't figure like Shiro—I know I have no blind spot here!"

Yes, there was no need to rush, thought Sora. Though he might not seek the Peach Blossom Spring, he could at the least drink of its lees! He imagined Steph washing Shiro's hair, Shiro meanwhile washing Izuna's tail...

...Though he could only go by the sound.

"Baths can go to hell, please."

"...Epic truf... But, right, now...denied."

"Once we finish this bath, you bitches gotta take me on, please. You better not flake, please."

"...Don't, worry; Brother...keeps, his promises..."

"I wonder. We speak of a man more skilled at lying than breathing."

"Oh, little Dora, do you not know of the holy scripture which says that it's your fault for falling for it?"

"What sort of fraudulent cult holds such scripture?"

" 'Tis scripture of my very own, compiled in my days of observing my masters. In consideration of its undoubtedly imminent status as holy scripture, I cannot conceive of a reason not to assign it such an appellation from the present time."

"I can conceive of a reason! Observing those two is just a pervert watch log!"

"......!"

Bear it. Bear it, Sora.

"Incidentally, sir, may I ask what you are doing?"

"Whuuuuuuhhhhhhhhh—aaaaaaaaaaaghhhhhhhhhh!!"

Popping up before Sora's eyes—a—a singularly well-muscled old body clad in only a loincloth— Ino caused Sora to raise his voice.

"Wh-what are you doing defiling the Peach Blossom Spring au naturel! There is no demand for geezer nudity!"

Oh, God... After all, I did calculate the camera placement perfectly, could it be this fart—? Surely he couldn't have been all big and bold right in front... If something like this was in the picture, any kind of hee-hee-hee clip would turn into a huh-huh-huh clip.

"Hmm, I heard that this was a rite of passage you established for new members of your party."

"It doesn't apply to dudes! Much less macho geezers! That's out of the question! I mean, what the hell are you doing coming in here all in the buff?! Didn't I say it's R-18?!"

"Well, I have been informed, but as of this year I am ninety-eight, which is eighty years older than the age limit."

"—Eh, uh, hmng? Wait, wha—?"

Hold on—we've just found an issue you can't overlook, Sora, virgin, eighteen. A certain issue, world-changing, yet too hot to touch—

"By the way, the honorable Jibril described to me this 'moral code' you seem to adhere to, sir..."

"Uh, yeah..."

Sora, thinking inside, *I would really prefer he kept this majestically imposing ripped body at a distance.* Just barely managed to squeeze out his answer.

"You see, I heard that you are eighteen years of age."

"Y-yeah, I guess."

"Then this would imply that you have the qualification to view materials that would be prohibited to those under eighteen years."

"Yeah, sure. And?"

Hmm, Ino went, stroking his beard, seeming lost in contemplation.

"Well, it occurred to me, if your concern is that you have Her Majesty Queen Shiro accompanying, would it not be the case that if you merely clothed and blindfolded *Queen Shiro*, there would be no need for shame were Your Majesty to enter into this scene freely?"

——The world stopped turning.

"Ah, aha-ha, aha-ha-ha-ha... Now then, now then, now-now-now wait a moment, lad."

"Yes, sir, what is it?"

"Th-th-there's no way I would overlook s-s-s-something so glaring; th-th-th-there's got to be something wrong, some mistake here."

"Hmm, that was in fact just the matter of my inquiry... But it puzzles you as well, sir?"

—*Tsk.* A soft but definite click entered Sora's ear. No, it couldn't have, not possibly. But he couldn't have misheard it, even more not possibly.

"E-excuse me, Ms. Shiro. I heard a click that said, 'Mind your own business, asshole,' but would you care to elucidate?"

He couldn't look at her. But Sora having addressed her based on a definite feeling that she was there, after a moment's pause:

"......I, didn't say, anything..."

"I'm sorry, Teacher, but I have absolute confidence that of all people I would not confuse your voice. I mean, come on, that click was totally you! Seriously, please, can I get an explanation—you thought of it?!"

"Hah-hah-hah... Is this what you call an epic fight?"

"Hey——hold on, you old fart! I almost missed it as you subjected me to shock after shock, but just whose sister are you looking at naked, you son of a bitch! You wanna have your eyeballs pulled out?"

"Oh, don't worry. I sympathize deeply with your provision that nude minors shall be banned from view. It is my belief that this is important to the moral education of Izuna as well, and thus I have my eyes tightly shut," said the old man.

So he could grasp his surroundings just fine with his sense of hearing alone? God damn these mutant assholes!

"...Mm, Izzy, you can't, look...at the others, either. Okay...?"

"? I don't get it, but understood, please."

"Wait, Ms. Shiro, please don't change the subject, yo— Wha—? I took countless Peach Blossom Springs and flushed them down the drain?!"

Sliding down to kneel by Sora's side, Jibril spoke.

"Master, I beg you to ease your heart. Surely it is not too late."

"R-really?"

"Yes, and with this knowledge, the solution is simple."

Spinning her finger around and around in space, drawing a circle of light, perhaps to perform magic.

"I, your humble slave Jibril, can envelop you and myself in spirits and block the flow of sound. If we but have Lady Shiro refrain from looking this way, considering that this body, to its every extremity, belongs to you, Master, you are free to do with it as you—"

"...Jibril...STF, U."

At Shiro's brief command, as she jointly held ownership of the Flügel with Sora, Jibril's mouth was shut. Right after, Shiro said sadly.

* * *

"—Brother, would you…blind…fold me, and…do dirty things…right, there?"

——……

"Haaaa-ha-ha-ha-ha-ha-ha! As if I'd do something so bad for my sister's moral education aah-hah-hah-hah-hah God daaaaaamn shiiiiiiiit buuurn it aaaalll dooowwwn aaaaaaaaaah!"

Sora having finally broken, his voice rang out throughout the bath.

"…By the way, sir."

"What do you want, old fart?! If you deepen the crack in my sanity any further—"

"Well, as of now, I belong to you."

"—Yeah. Not that that's a line I wanna hear from a macho old guy in a loincloth."

Having apparently been afflicted by goose bumps for a moment, Sora's comeback was grim. Ino, nevertheless, gave no indication of breaking his smile.

"And Izuna also belongs to you—having acknowledged these things, may I comment?"

With a sunny grin, his eyes still closed, only his voice lowering, Ino asked.

"—Just *what in the hell did you tell* Izuna, you hairless monkey?"

…The "way so no one would die" Sora had whispered to Izuna. There was no way there could be anything so convenient. Toward the con artist who had dangled an empty comfort before his granddaughter, more important than his own life, yet as one whose rights had all been forfeit, to whom no resistance was permitted, this was the old man's one small gesture of defiance. Without even turning, Sora dismissively—

"…Just shut up, suck your thumb, and watch, Gramps. It's not like you can do anything."

—picked the perfect response to get the old man's goat, trolling him. At this, Ino's already clenched his fists tightened, but at Sora's subsequent words, instead of anger—

* * *

"Relax—*there's still a surprise at the end.* Once you see that, you'll know the answer."

Sora teased with a bold smile—and it seemed to Ino, an eerie one. At the words of the man hinting at a plot even beyond what had come before, Ino, feeling now more fearful than angry, was left speechless...

CHAPTER 4
RULE NUMBER 10

CONVERGENCE

The Kingdom of Elkia. The capital, Elkia. Elkia Royal Castle. Another day with the monarch siblings sitting on the throne, busy with their games. But, today, there was one new face.

"—Why—why can't I beat you assholes, please?!"

Thus shouting, tearing at her black hair, sitting in front of the throne, was a young animal-eared girl in traditional Japanese-style clothing: Izuna. In her hands was a DSP, the game system Sora and Shiro had brought from another world.

"Hah-hah-hah, these are games we brought from our world. We've even analyzed all the variables like a goddamn TASer; we've *maxed* 'em all out, literally. You think you can beat us that easily?"

"...Izzy, if this...discourages you...you've got, a long way..."

Sora and Shiro, laughing at her, had one side of their DSP in Shiro's had as she sat in Sora's lap, while Sora operated the other side, playing in the manner of a three-legged race. This situation necessitated by the fact that Sora and Shiro had each brought only one system from their old world. Though normally this would have been a handicap, for Sora and Shiro, it allowed them to show their full potential.

"Like hell I'm discouraged, please! Come on, one more time, please!"

"Sure thing. We'll take you on as many times as you want, right, Shiro?"

"...Izzy...you rely, too much...on your eyes. You, gotta...read ahead..."

"Hey, Shiro, don't spoil Izuna like that! That's the kinda thing you gotta learn for yourself!"

Into the boisterous throne room burst a person of ghastly visage.

"So—So-So-So—Sora! They got us!"

—Steph had for the past few days been running around frantically, facilitating the incorporation of the continental domain into Elkia. As Steph flew in short of breath—*hff, hff*—Sora raised his eyes from his portable game.

"Oh, what is it, Steph?"

"Why are you all relaxed? They got us! The Eastern Union!"

Seeing Steph obviously out of sorts, Sora merely smiled thinly and spoke.

"So before the game, the Eastern Union *pulled all their major personnel and technology out of their continental domain*—did they?"

"...Uh huh...uh?"

...That was it exactly. Having been told exactly the news she was trying to convey, Steph froze. Yes—the Eastern Union had indeed, per the covenant, delivered to Immanity "everything on the continent." However, now it had become clear that as of the start of the game, the Eastern Union had already taken the technology and machines that Immanity would need to make use of the land the Eastern Union had developed and utilized and *moved them off the continent.* Indeed, it did not infringe upon the covenant. Sora was the one who had demanded "everything on the continent," and as such, anything not on the continent would not be included. But as Sora laughed even this off, Steph whispered.

"You—you knew?"

As usual, not taking his eyes off his game, he answered absently.

"Yeah, I mean—*that's why* I said 'everything on the continent,' right?"

"—Wh-what do you mean? What are we supposed to do with this territory now?"

Then they'd only taken back the borders of the continental domain. They could barely do anything with the farms and other facilities that the Eastern Union had developed. It was true that the knowledge Sora and Shiro had brought from their world could address it, given enough time. But considering the food financing crisis Elkia faced, these resources definitely would have helped. But Sora mumbled shortly thereafter.

"Eh, don't worry—*the game's not over.*"

"Not—not over…?"

After going through that kind of hell, it was *not over*—? As Steph considered whether, depending on the meaning of his statement, it might be advisable to give him a good faint.

"…King Sora, may I have a moment?"

Yet another person appeared in the Presence Chamber. A traditionally-clad, aging, white-haired Werebeast—Ino Hatsuse.

"Oh, here you are; I was waiting for you."

"It sounds as though you knew why I was here."

"It's not 'as though'—I *know.* You've got a letter from the Eastern Union, right?"

"Y-yes…delivered using the fastest service…"

Sora opened the letter he was handed. It was written in Immanity. In contrast to Shiro, who studied it, Sora just glanced.

"Jibril."

"I am here."

Jibril answering Sora's call by materializing out thin air to kneel before him.

"You can shift to the capital of the Eastern Union, right?"

"Yes, I can—but how did you know?"

As Jibril gaped, puzzled, an amused Sora continued without explanation.

"We got a call—straight from the Shrine Maiden, the agent plenipotentiary of the Eastern Union, so here we go."

At Sora's careless declaration, Ino and even Izuna, who had been playing a game, stopped their hands and stretched open their eyes.

"Th-the Holy Shrine Maiden—has summoned you?!"

"Yeah, what, is that, like, a big deal or something?"

"A big deal—?"

—The "Shrine Maiden." The one whose true name no one knew, who had brought together the Eastern Union from a mere collection of countless island tribes. The one who had elevated them to the status of third-greatest country in the world in a mere half century, a god among beasts. She—had called upon them directly? But Jibril answered that with disbelief of an entirely different nature.

"It is what you should call a 'big deal,' Master. Now that the tables are turned and they have been cut off from their continental resources, for them to summon you is a ludicrous proposition. If they have business with you, good sense would dictate that they come themselves."

At Jibril, beaming as she said this, Ino and Izuna thrust a glare. It spoke to the Shrine Maiden's status among Werebeast. But Sora—

"Nah, see, they must be asking us 'cause they know we've got you, Jibril. In other words—they've got something so urgent they need us to come stat, get it?"

As Sora chuckled, Ino, hesitatingly, said once again.

"—It sounds as though you know why she calls."

But Sora just flashed a smile, grabbed Shiro from his lap under his shoulder, stood, and ordered:

"Come, clutch onto Jibril and let us go! To the paradise of this world—the animal-girl empire!"

In answer to these words, Jibril spread her wings.

"Now—this will be a long-distance shift, ladies and gentlemen, so please hang on. Please sit up in your seats and fasten your seat belts securely. Should you experience nausea during the shift, unless you are one of my two masters, please take advantage of the compartments of your clothing. Ah, but Masters, please feel free to—"

"...Jibril, enough of that; come on, let's go."

Jibril displayed the array of knowledge she had acquired from Sora's tablet, but Sora hurried her, fidgeting as if he couldn't bear the siren's song of the animal-eared kingdom.

"Please forgive me, Master. A long-distance shift such as this requires some preparation."

With this, Jibril opened her wings wider. Her geometric halo increased the speed of its revolution dramatically, and her palely sparkling feathers clearly emitted light. Everything started to warp as if in a heat haze—and space began to fold.

"—!"

"This—can't...!"

Izuna and Ino each used their hands not touching Jibril to cover an ear against the torment. Sora and the other Immanities, unable to sense magic at all, felt suffocated, as if the air had been compressed. It was beyond their ability to know how it felt to the Werebeasts, whose senses were sharp enough to pick up magic. But if someone who could clearly use magic—say Fi had been here, then probably...

...she'd faint from all the spirits that conglomerated and surrounded them. And then Jibril, her amber eyes open slightly—clearly not looking here but *someplace far away*—said:

"With that, ladies and gentlemen, we will be on our way to Kannagari, capital of the Eastern Union—landing in the Inner Garden of the Central Division of the Shrine."

Upon Jibril's casual declaration that she'd jump right into the heart of the Shrine, Ino—

"Distance: 4,527.21 kilometers. Time to destination: 0.023 seconds. It is expected that for the two Werebeasts onboard, it will be an exceedingly uncomfortable flight, so please relax and enjoy the trip."

—there was no chance to speak. As as a sound like glass shattering assailed their ears, like photos in a slide show—

—their surroundings flipped.

"Agh..."

Holding his head which ached slightly, perhaps a side effect of the long-distance shift, Sora looked around.

—It was a place somehow reminiscent of the Japanese gardens of their old world. Wooden buildings suggesting Southeast Asia enclosing them. All that lit them under the black sky was reddish lamplight. Jibril had apparently jumped right into the middle of the Shrine, but the shrine grounds must have been extensive for just barely visible beyond the structures and fences surrounding them was what appeared to be a city. Countless high-rise buildings, emitting the red flickering of paper lanterns. Trees blocked the light to create a pattern of irregular black contrast that swept across the scene.

"Oh, I get it. It's a different time zone."

Sora realized, a little late, that it was night.

"—What's this?"

Then something caught his eye: Izuna and Ino, keeled over on the ground. Shiro and Steph, also holding their slightly aching heads, imitated Sora as they looked around. Jibril stood with her hands together before her, as if to convey wordlessly to her lords, *We have arrived.*

"...Hey, Jibril, what's up with Izuna and Ino?"

"As I mentioned, I expect that the trip was *remarkably uncomfortable* for the Werebeasts, with their fine senses. Perhaps what we are seeing is the effect of hearing the super-ultra-high frequencies created when *a hole is opened in space.*"

"...Hmm, I'm glad we as a race are just dense enough not to get how nuts you are."

Holding his ears, Ino stood up with a pained face that suggested a swollen blood vessel.

"What are you, a disaster on wings?! Use some common sense in mocking the laws of physics, you antique bitch! And then you barge right into our Maiden's Holy Shrine without authorization! Just how far do you intend to screw with us, you little shit?!"

Sora chastised the screaming Ino, while secretly thinking to himself, "Is that something you want to word as a question?"

"Old man, keep a lid on it. I mean, cool it. It's just—"

Though thoroughly disgusted by Ino's outburst, Sora quickly changed his tune when Izuna painfully muttered moments later:

"...This blows, please... I wanna barf, please."

"Jibril, think of Izzy! What are you doing to one of the world's greatest treasures?!"

"Ah, I do apologize, Master! Frankly, those other than my masters never even entered my consideration! I repent!"

Ignoring this commotion, Shiro and Steph took in their surroundings.

"...This, is...the Eastern Union?"

"Quite old buildings for such an advanced civilization. With that sort of an embassy, I thought—"

Jibril answered their mumblings.

"This Shrine itself was built 920 years ago. If you exit, you will find a number of fascinating buildings which include high-rises such as the embassy. As I can best gather from the tablet, to put it in terms of my masters' world—what we have here is the culture of the 1900s."

Sora called up the knowledge from his memory. When he'd seen the embassy of the Eastern Union in Elkia, his first impression had been of something akin to the Empire State Building, which was built probably sometime around 1930, and that it was representative of their architectural state of the art.

"...And yet they have perfect VR in their games. Shit."

"Now then, Master, though this may remind you of your world, you must remember it is a different civilization."

Unable to accept the fantasy elements, the groaning Sora went on.

"Hang on, Jibril. You sure know a lot here. From books?"

"That is one factor, but also I've flown over the Eastern Union many times."

To Jibril as she declared this with a smile, Ino shouted as if still holding a grudge.

"How many times must I tell you it's a *violation of our airspace*?!"

"I beg your pardon, sir, but if you intend to make such declarations, I suggest that first you develop flight technology so that you can reasonably claim *control of the airspace.* I might also add that, considering that we have been summoned by the Holy Shrine Maiden (lol), it hardly strikes me a violation. If it were, then surely the Covenants would disable its execution?"

"Hey, you greasy pigeon! There was clearly an insinuation in the way you mentioned the Holy Shrine Maiden just now! Why don't you—"

As the bickering continued, suddenly from out of the darkness:

"...Oh, my. Aren't you all having a jolly old time. Might I be included?"

—*Ring.* Soft like a bell drifted in the dulcet tones of old Kyoto, stilling the group's exchange.

—How long had she been there? A bewitchingly golden girl sat on the railing of a red bridge over a garden pond. Wearing the kind of garb expected of a shrine maiden, woven of the three colors of white, red, and black, a golden...two-tailed fox. In the garden lit only by the moon and the vermillion lamplight, the long hair and ears that asserted that she was a Werebeast glistened all the more strongly. Her eyes, which were like gold itself—full of inorganic light, reflected images of Sora and Shiro.

"You from Elkia, who have come from beyond the sea, welcome to the light of the spirit of the moon—O king and queen of *people*. I'm the lady of this garden—heh, the one they call the Shrine Maiden. A pleasure."

The Shrine Maiden, smiling disarmingly with her cheek supported by her forearm. This was the agent plenipotentiary of the Eastern Union—practically speaking, the queen of Werebeasts. At the sight of her, Izuna and Ino promptly got down on the ground and lowered their heads.

"O-o Holy Shrine Maiden, I beg you to forgive our gross misconduct. Having allowed the continent to be taken, even our selves to be taken, and ultimately this outrage, I know nothing I can say or do—"

"W-we're real sorry, please…"

"I-Izuna! Talk in Werebeast, not Immanity! Who do you think you're talking—?"

"Ah dear, how tiresome. Relax. I'll be exhausted ere too long."

As the two Werebeasts deferred with all their might, Sora regardless stood proud as ever.

"Woo, you're the Shrine Maiden? Man, you look the part. Hey, hey, can I get a pic?"

—But how could her beauty be captured with a cell phone camera? Sora cursed himself for not bringing a DSLR. Meanwhile, a panicked Steph stammeringly attempted to upbraid him.

"H-hey, this is an ultra-important foreign dignitary here! Mind a few manners, would you!"

But the siblings and Jibril all gaped at the kneeling Steph blankly.

"Huh, why? Isn't the host the one who has to lower her head?"

As Shiro and Jibril nodded to indicate perfect agreement with Sora's interpretation of the etiquette of the situation, Steph held her head from a pain that was clearly not the result of teleportation. Seemingly without paying much notice to this exchange, the Shrine Maiden pleasantly and courteously capitulated.

"You certainly are an amusing lot… Well, 'tis true I was the one who called upon you. I suppose I should be greeting you properly on my knees with my head low—

"—but when I've called you to complain, can you understand how bowing my head might be difficult?"

"Oh? I can't really remember doing anything to give you cause for complaint."

In contrast to Ino and Steph, who wanted to scream *How dare you?*, the Shrine Maiden merely countered in a tone reminiscent of wind chimes.

"Aye… Well then, shall I put it to you straight?"

Her golden eyes, narrowed by her smile, were narrowed for another reason as well.

"You've really *done it now*, you hairless monkeys."

The Shrine Maiden delivered this insult without even compromising either her grace or refinement, prompting in Sora an ironic smile.

"Ha-ha, so they did. Nice, Elf. You guys work faster than I thought."

Those who understood what he meant were Sora, Shiro, and Jibril. And Izuna—who had been filled in later, probably alone. At the bewildered Ino and Steph, the Shrine Maiden only sighed as if laughing.

"Well, I imagine you know by now, but without the continent, we can't do anything. We've got to get it back if it costs us our lives. If we don't, our administration and finance will be in shambles. Even so, to mount a challenge from our side— Eh, you know it's no good. And another thing—"

Grinning frivolously, Sora finished her words.

"Just in case, you moved your core technology and engineers, key staff and vital materials off the continent."

—Yes. As if in answer to Steph's gaze, wondering how he knew, Sora explained.

"That's what anyone with half a brain would do first if someone demanded the whole continental domain. For insurance."

With a little chuckle and a nod, the Shrine Maiden continued.

"There can be no value in land you can't steer, so Elkia has to come challenge us to another game if they want the tech to use it. You've got no choice. The rest is simple: You fall into our hands and get your rump pounded, roasted, and served."

—In other words, they'd bring them into a game where no monitoring could enter, a game full of all the cheats they wanted, and finish them off for sure. But…the Shrine Maiden finished, cheek in hand, with a cloudy grin that said, "You got us."

"—But *you knew* I'd figure that, didn't you?"

"Of course. I mean, that's what I do."

"Aye…that you would use so little time so well…"

The Shrine Maiden sighed.

"That you had the forethought while we were pulling our important materials off the continent to make contact with Elf—and to expose our game through a spy…to use Elven Gard to lay siege to the Eastern Union, good heavens."

"Sorry, we're starving bums with no time to spare."

"Wha—"

Ino stood dumbfounded. But let's go ahead and say it—this wasn't the time to be going dumb.

"—Righto, but *I saw that coming, too,* you know?"

Now it was the Shrine Maiden's turn to stare back at Sora smugly.

"Never mind that I took you yourselves for agents of Elven Gard."

"Guess you would. Definitely more sensible than believing someone who says they're from another world."

"Aye, it's a sensible idea. Indeed, getting hung up on it must've been what led to my downfall."

With a *heh*, the Shrine Maiden closed her eyes and turned her face to the sky.

"—So when Avant Heim showed up, that was the end for us."

Now this was the appropriate moment—Ino went dumb and shifted his gaze. Jibril, her eyes also closed, stood wordlessly as if in awe of her master's stratagem. *Gulp*, swallowed Ino. Just when—when in the world had he fallen into this trap? But judging by the Shrine Maiden's account, Sora had had it all set up *from the beginning.* Which meant… By the time he'd come to Ino, he'd already—

(This is a battle of wits between one who intends to swallow up the world and one who's built the third-largest country in half a century...) Ino shivered.

—Yes, Jibril was on the Council of Eighteen Wings—a member of Avant Heim's government. Though she might have been excluded from her seat having become Sora's property, that didn't remove her clout. All they had to do was ask her to give Flügel this simple message:

—"We've uncovered the Eastern Union's secret. If you want their knowledge, we'll tell you how to beat them." As for the rest, knowing those knowledge-thirsty Flügel, the result—didn't need to be spelled out.

As if cross she'd been outwitted, the Shrine Maiden dangled her legs with a pouty smile. Bonking her wooden sandals against the bridge railing, the golden fox spoke sulkily.

"Elven Gard, Avant Heim. And Elkia... Under siege by so many nations with their shields together, our game exposed plain as daylight—no struggle can save us from this... Ah, dear me."

She quit her repetitive clomping, kicking off lightly from the bridge railing upon which she sat.

"...As such—"

That one movement was enough to instantly close the distance between Sora's group and the golden fox. With those inscrutable eyes of hers, she peered into Sora's.

"The Eastern Union, as of now—challenges Elkia to an immediate reprisal."

"Wha—?!"

Ino doubted his ears while Izuna kept her eyes downcast. As far as Ino knew, the Eastern Union had no way to take the offensive. Even if they did, their opponent—was Sora and Shiro. Who had defeated Flügel. Who had legitimately defeated the Eastern Union at their own games. The Werebeasts were hardly in a position to initiate a challenge against those two at all, even assuming that there was the slightest chance of victory— But the Shrine Maiden continued, her expression a mask of resolve as if she were well aware of the circumstances.

"This is the man who's blocked off our escape, eh? Now that our hand's open, we can't even defend anymore. It's only a matter of time before he concocts all manner of tricks to create a situation in which we have no choice but to ask for a game."

"...Just like you did to Elf and Flügel— Now you're trapped."

The Shrine Maiden laughing mirthlessly as Sora grinned from ear to ear.

"Shall I be frank? Of the three countries we now face, the only one we still have a chance at beating is Immanity—Elkia."

Even that mirthless laugh fading—

"And you have the bait of our assets and technology. We must reclaim what you took so our country can stand. Else we'll be in the gutter, poised for destruction... Shall I say it again, lad?

"You really did it now, you hairless monkeys—*we won't die without a fight, I'll have you know.*"

From the Shrine Maiden, glaring daggers at Sora as if to stab him to death, there was no longer any tone of conviviality. Only an extraordinary determination—to kill—radiating toward the man before her.

—*If we're going to die, we're taking you scum with us!*— At this lethal mood pervading the very air, Ino's spine froze. The Eastern Union. The third-largest country in the world. A race a full two ranks above Immanity. (This man immobilized us in a single move?!)

—At this unbelievable scenario, his hair stood on end. The plotting that transcended wisdom. The calculation like a devil's. The malice, the hostility the Shrine Maiden exuded. Though such thoughts were impertinent, disgraceful—still, Ino could only see it now as futile clambering. The Shrine Maiden, the living legend, who had built up the world's third-greatest nation in only half a century.

Now everything she had created was poised to crumble—at a single move by a mere pair of Immanities. But bearing her gaze head-on, Sora opened his mouth.

"Oh that, that... That's the part I don't get..."

Words that took the air, swelled like a balloon, and deflated the tension in an instant.

"Why should I destroy this awesomest-in-the-world animal-eared paradise?!"

Dumbstruck at these words: Ino, Steph, and—the Shrine Maiden herself.

"This is animal-girls we're talking about! Here we've got a butt-load of super-cute furries, and to top it off, a hot golden fox shrine maiden! D00d, the very fact you exist is a cheat!! What kind of fail-sauce would that be if I were to destroy this worldly treasure?! Losing Werebeast would be a loss for the world...for culture! What the hell is even wrong with that asshat Tet for not putting you on a protected species list?!"

——. The surrounding atmosphere suddenly devoid of all hostility. Ino, Steph—and even the Shrine Maiden—could only stare in shock.

"So with that in mind—what was it, 'reprisal,' you said? Sure thing, let's do it."

With these words, Sora took out—a coin.

"Even I'm tired of playing all those complex diplomatic games by now. Let's just get this over with, shall we?"

The game he suggested with the coin—was clear.

"I'll toss the coin. You call heads or tails before it falls. I'll take the other side. If I win, the Eastern Union's gonna be annexed into Elkia. What do you think?"

Sora showed both sides of the coin as he spoke.

"I'm the one who declared the reprisal. You're the ones who get to decide the game... But a coin toss, really?"

"What, you got a problem?"

At Sora's dismissive smile, the Shrine Maiden raised a voice and a grin.

"—Nah, it's fine."

"To think the country I built up over half a century, half my life, should be yanked from its foundations by a pair of hairless monkeys, heh-heh… And the arbiter of its end…is a coin toss—eh-ha-ha-ha!"

Holding her stomach as she laughed breathlessly, the Shrine Maiden thought:

—*Should be fun in a way, and there's no turning back.* They were playing Immanity, just as she'd mentioned, the only opponent against which they still had the slightest chance. And the game that they proposed…of all things…was a coin toss. No matter what kind of tricks were employed, Werebeast's—the Shrine Maiden's—senses could see through everything in this game. And on top of that, they'd said *she could pick the side she liked* after the toss.

—How amusing. If she were to lose under these conditions, it was a done deal…that the Eastern Union was on its way to ruin anyway. Switching to a fearless grin, the Shrine Maiden spoke.

"Why not. Let's play this game of yours."

Sora looked back at this with amusement. As if—yes—as if watching a comrade.

"I knew you were one of *us*. I like you more and more."

"My demand, mind—is that you guarantee the rights of Werebeast and give us the right of self-government and resources from the continent."

The one who'd made the challenge…was the Shrine Maiden, so there was no point in asking for impossible demands he'd just dismiss. Instead, she'd go high risk, low return, but still as far as she could get away with. The Shrine Maiden calculated that this demand was it. To ask for the continental resources to be "returned" was the same as denying the preceding first match entirely. Now that they'd seized the initiative, her choices—were all too limited.

—But if she could at least secure a guarantee of Werebeasts' rights...

"If you can just get us to guarantee the rights of Werebeast, then you'll at least be able to get back the Werebeasts left on the continent. And then you'll have a foothold from which to take back your resources—yeah, those are some Shrine Maiden skills you got."

Sora answered the Shrine Maiden's demand with a smile that seemed to say, "*You pass.*" (The bloke's seen through everything?)

"Well, then—shall we proceed with what is probably the maddest coin toss the world has ever seen?"

"You're quite amusing, lad... Would you mind terribly if I had a say in your demand?"

"Depends what you've got?"

"Swear you won't mistreat Izuna or Ino—or my people. *Even if you get the Werebeast Piece.*"

—Yes, if the Eastern Union was annexed into Elkia...the agency of the Eastern Union, currently held by the Shrine Maiden—would automatically pass to Sora and Shiro. What lay beyond that was servitude or oppression... In any case, they had no future save ruin—that was what it meant to *lose the Race Piece.* To these final words from the Shrine Maiden, Sora's expression clearly indicated, "*This time you fail.*"

"—You still don't get it? Eh, whatever—*Aschente.*"

"*Aschente*—let's go."

And so, perhaps the highest-risk coin toss in history. Started—with a *clink* from Sora's hand.

■■■

The moment the coin resounded from Sora's hand. The golden Shrine Maiden's eyes and fur—were stained red like an exploding paint balloon.

"—Wha…?!"

Utter shock as, most likely, no one there had known that the Shrine Maiden was capable of "bloodbreak."

—Yet while Sora and Shiro treated it as nothing, everyone else raised their voices.

(Well, let's let 'em see how futile my struggling *is*, shall we?) At the same instant her blood splattered, the Shrine Maiden's subjective world came to a standstill. The entirety of her psyche accelerated—her keenly honed senses, her sixth sense, even her perception of magic—reading everything.

—One magic response. From the Flügel before her. But none of that prickly sensation of a rite being woven. Only the fetal movements of spirits that arose by virtue of a Flügel's presence. No one there was using magic—meaning there was no magical impropriety. (But it can't be the lad's got nothing up his sleeve, can it?) In the mind of the smirking Shrine Maiden, once more, the world snapped.

—With a sound that went *whapow*…her awareness, already expanded by her bloodbreak, further expanded to a range that threatened to destroy her. Her senses, exceeding the limits of physics—grasped everything within a five-hundred-meter radius. A force field—breaking out the spiritual boundaries of the shrine. The space in a radius of five hundred meters that had become the Shrine Maiden's world: everything that existed there—every leaf and grain of sand—she felt move, held in her hands, so close she could count them. (No magic response anywhere here—not even from the… coin?) Suspicion spread through the Shrine Maiden's heart.

—The Shrine Maiden's senses encompassed the drafts of wind, the dust that drifted in it, each individual particle. The revolution speed of the coin was stable. Magical tricks were not in play. But the coin did trace a course sufficiently regular that she could tell it had been tossed in a deliberate fashion. Indeed, it traced exactly the path she had expected and fell. Which meant—after 142⅔ revolutions, it would hit the floor, and after four rebounds and 5.2 seconds of spinning—it would come up tails. It was obvious that Sora

had tossed it *so that it would.* (For the lad to underestimate so my vision for moving objects, my senses…would be implausible.) After the game with Izuna, this man could hardly misunderstand a Werebeast's senses. But assuming there was no trick, the coin would definitely land tails. As long as the Shrine Maiden answered *tails*, if it didn't come up tails, there was an impropriety for sure. Which she had no mind to overlook. But—with Sora's heartbeat, Shiro's heartbeat, the response of the spirits in Jibril's body—and…*even Izuna*—pounding regularly to indicate certainty in Sora's victory, what was she to make of it. Answer heads or tails before it started to fall?

—Why wait?

"…Tails, lad."

The recoil from having exceeded her limits barraged her body at the same time as she recalled her bloodbreak. This wasn't a game world as with Izuna; it was a bloodbreak in reality. Just as the name indicated. It would break her blood—in some cases even take her life with the power it cost. If she used that and still lost…

(—A right ass I'd be. 'Twould be a droll jest if aught.) The coin, arcing gently, beginning to fall.

—If it was tails, the Shrine Maiden would win. If it was heads, foul play would be proven, and Sora would lose. All she'd have to do was present the evidence, and then Sora shouldn't have a snowball's chance in hell of winning. Opening eyes clouded by the recoil from her bloodbreak, taking care not to miss the moment of falsehood. And as the coin turned gracefully—

—it fell toward the stone pavement, hit the stone, and—

—*stayed.* Wedged between the stones—on end.

……

——……What?

"Oh my God, does this mean it's a draw?! Like, holy shit, amirite?!"

At Sora's insincere query, everyone but Ino, Steph, and the Shrine

Maiden—even Izuna, who until that moment had had her head downcast—let out a smile.

"Whoa, man. If the coin *stands*, does it mean we both win or we both lose?"

Theatrically, Sora put his hand to his chin and acted as if thinking as he asked.

"If we both win—it means both of our demands go through, so then...? You come under Elkia's umbrella, yet Werebeast gets guaranteed rights, continued self-governance, and a share in the continental resources...so it's like...

"The Eastern Union becomes part of the 'Commonwealth' of Elkia, right? ♥"

As Sora blithely proposed a *multiracial national federation*, the Shrine Maiden found herself at a loss for words.

—The Shrine Maiden knew. That Sora *knew that the stone he was standing on could move* and stood there intentionally. Tossing the coin so that just before it fell—he could shift his weight upon the stone a bit and let the coin fall into the gap. A blatantly—practically insultingly—obvious "impropriety." By the Ten Covenants, an impropriety discovered meant a loss. All the Shrine Maiden had to do was point it out, and she would win. But a *question* that assailed the Shrine Maiden prevented her from making the point—

"My—my dear...you... Aren't you giving me more than I sought?!"

...Yes, were she to accept the "win-win" Sora had presented, the Shrine Maiden would walk away with more than she'd asked while Sora's benefit from his demand would fade. However one looked at it, he was cheating to the Shrine Maiden's—to the Eastern Union's—advantage.

—For that reason, the Shrine Maiden couldn't easily point out his duplicity. She had to figure out Sora's true motive—but the king of Immanity just continued playfully.

"Uhh, so you're saying a girl probably lording it over the Eastern

Union, a smart chick so über-hot she's like the alpha and the omega, still *won't frickin' listen*? So now she's got the clumsy-girl status, too, making her basically a *moe* goddess?!"

—Won't…frickin'…listen? Had she, out of the entire assemblage, missed something? The Shrine Maiden widened her eyes, reviewed everything that had led up to the present. And immediately these words caught. *This is animal-girls we're talking about?! Here we've got a buttload of* super-cute furries, *and to top it off, a hot golden fox shrine maiden. D00d, the very fact you exist is a cheat—*

—*"So, with that in mind"—*

"…You…were always…?"

"Huh, what's this now? I mean, you want it to be win-win? Or you want it to be lose-lose? *Which do you prefer?*"

Sora twisted his body frivolously and put the question to the gaping Shrine Maiden.

(…He really… He really had me dancing to his tune from start to finish… I see now.) The Shrine Maiden, muttering silently—found herself out of options. In all likelihood, no one would ask *why* by this point, but the Shrine Maiden chuckled to herself and thought. (It…goes without sayin'…) If these people—*came to win for real…* her confidence she could win was nonexistent.

"…You dirty knave… Let's say it's win-win, then."

Smiling thusly, she sat down on a nearby rock out of the exhaustion from the bloodbreak, and she clutched her belly.

"Heh-heh, hee-hee-hee! You really…you really amuse me! You wags! Eh-ha-ha-ha-ha!"

What a joke, what a joke of a game. What a joke of a trick! What a farce of a fraud! These rascals who'd wagged the Eastern Union, wagged Werebeast—wagged me! Good Lord! They'd taken her so sweepingly, all the Shrine Maiden could do was laugh. Even her doubtful *Can I really trust these folks?*—had flown. If this had been Sora's aim from the very beginning, his *true purpose*—was plain to see.

—That is. (This chap doesn't even—want the Werebeast Piece.) That could mean…only one thing.

This man—truly intended to take on the God. And that was why he realized.

—A Race Piece…was *not to be taken*—

And, thereupon—with the fullest of smiles, Sora stretched grandly.

"Mmmmm! So basically, we become the 'Commonwealth of Elkia.' Can I take it *we're good*?"

Having come this far, still—with a face that said he'd give the Shrine Maiden a special shocking jack-in-the-box—Sora spoke.

"You know Elven Gard? We *used the Covenants to alter their informant's memories before she reported.* Elven Gard's—heard the Eastern Union's game wrong."

"Wha—…?"

With that, Sora stuck up his thumb and stuck out his tongue, and with an expression that alleviated all the tension a funny face could, he casually uttered something unbelievable.

"So—I'm—saying, when those d00ds come for you, lead 'em on—*and then kick their asses.* ♥ Might even help you out if you give me a call… Hit me up; we'll separate those fools from their territory, yeah?"

—At this point, finally, Steph and Ino understood. The *true reason* Chlammy and Fi—*had had to be there.* To study the Eastern Union for foul play, to *bluff* that they had the Eastern Union on its knees, and furthermore—to undermine.

(—Even this, was part—of the game?) What crossed Steph's mind was a resounding "yes," as she recalled Sora's assertion before coming here that "the game's not over."

"Oh, and Avant Heim, that was just something Jibril instigated using her clout. The nation itself doesn't have any ill will toward the Eastern Union. Anyway, we're in the countdown before Avant Heim falls under Elkia's umbrella, so you can just ignore them… Anyhoo—"

Sora, having successfully baffled everyone gathered there, firing off one incredible utterance after the other, finally let out one big breath so as to move on.

"—And——so! We're good, right? This wraps it all up, right? Right?"

Steph could not help but comment on the manner is which her master fidgeted at this last line.

"Wh—why you so nervous?"

It was as if she'd triggered a land mine.

"Whaat?! Why the hell do you think I went through all this tedious bullshit?!"

Like a broken dam, Sora poured out his heart.

"I did it all so I'd get to *pet animal-girls*! I can't take it anymore! Shrine Maiden!"

"Uh, eh, what?"

"It is time you allow us to pet you!"

"...Pet you—!"

Sora and Shiro scrutinized the Shrine Maiden with steel in their eyes. Still, she responded with a very kind smile.

"While you may pet me as you like by mutual consent, long as you do no harm—*I'll pass.*"

"You—what?!"

"You should have thrown in the unconditional right to pet me with that coin toss... Now if you wish to pet me, you'll have to take me on again?"

As the Shrine Maiden grinned ear to ear, crossing her legs on the crag, Sora asked hastily:

"—Y-yo, Jibril, what time is it now?!"

"Sir—let's see... It is around eight o'clock."

...Crap! If he started playing the Shrine Maiden again now, there wouldn't be time!

"Damn, we have no choice! Let's hit the town and pet some animal-girls, Shiro!"

"...Golden...sparkly fox...fluffy...!"

Nghh, Shiro reached out her hands for the Shrine Maiden as Sora dragged the reluctant girl away.

"Fear not, Shiro, this is not a surrender! We shall return in order to discuss self-government within the Commonwealth and other bor—sorry, important matters! Prepare—to have your ears and tail petted, Holy Shrine Maiden!!"

Sora made this declaration with a finger smashed toward the Shrine Maiden, apparently convinced. Shiro's eyes glinted keenly as she followed Sora's lead in bashing out a finger.

"...Get, ready, bitch... We'll, fluff you up...!"

Picking up Shiro and running, Sora called over his shoulder by way of an aside.

"Oh, Steph, we're not coming back to Elkia until we're satisfied, so take care of the country for us!"

"Huh?"

Sora and Shiro noisily dashed away at full speed, yelling chaotically. Jibril followed uninstinctively, and Steph panicked and chased after them.

"Wai—! This must be a joke, some sort of jest! I'm already dying working to incorporate the continental domain, so surely you don't mean to dump the entire task of establishing an unprecedented multiracial commonwealth on me! Do you?!"

And so—the calm after the storm enveloped the garden. Izuna flicked her gaze restlessly after the departed tempest called Sora and Shiro as they faded into the distance. Composing herself once more, the Shrine Maiden broke the silence with her voice like bells.

"...Ino Hatsuse, Izuna Hatsuse."

"Y-yes, Your Holiness!"

"What do you want, please?"

"I said, Izuna, how dare you!"

"Now that both our demands have gone through—your possession has been released."

—Yes, the *guarantee of the rights of Werebeast*. Now that Sora had taken that on, the two were no longer the property of Elkia. However—

"—As the Shrine Maiden, agent plenipotentiary of Werebeast, I command you. Go with them."

"Understood, please!"

No sooner had the Shrine Maiden issued her orders than Izuna was tilting full speed after Sora and Shiro without asking for further explanation. Meanwhile...Ino wondered: was she telling them to *spy*?

"Learn as much as you can from that amusing lot. 'The way of the weak' and all. Also..."

The precaution slid from the Shrine Maiden's lips informed mirthfully from her heart.

"Mind you don't make enemies of those two."

—Just as Sora and Shiro had promised, they would no doubt return in the coming days to flesh out the details of the "Commonwealth." And certainly, they would challenge her to settle issues by means of the Covenants. And almost as certainly—she would lose. The Shrine Maiden considered this with something approaching conviction...and a chuckle.

"I've never felt so glad someone wasn't my enemy. These folks truly—"

And with a face that seemed to speak to something more fun than she'd ever experienced in her life. With a gaze full of giddy anticipation. Watching the backs of Sora and company as they left, the Shrine Maiden spoke:

"—might take down Tet himself, you know?"

■■■

The street was lined with architecture that to Sora and Shiro felt a mite old-fashioned, nostalgic. The neighborhood lit in lantern scarlet, in fantastic neon.

"...King Sora."

"Huh?! Don't tell me you're gonna get in the way of our petting spree, old fart."

Ino caught up with Sora and Shiro a step faster than Izuna. At the sight of the two promptly setting about molesting a bunny-girl, he momentarily fumbled for words.

"...Your swiftness inspires awe, sir, but have you obtained proper consent?"

"Hnh? Oh, yeah. I don't know what the deal is, but all Izuna has to do is tell all the girls around, 'These assholes are damn good at petting, please,' and they all just let us pet them. I wonder why?"

Watching a rabbit-eared Werebeast let out a *Hffmmm*, Ino thought—

—that he knew the reason. No one ever before had *had the petting skills to make Izuna sigh aloud*. This was a famous anecdote at large within the Eastern Union. If Izuna said they were good—

"...Well, there is just one thing that puzzles me."

Wary of the idea of telling them this, Ino went about his original question.

"Okay, sure, make it quick. We're in a hurry here!"

To Sora, who answered without stopping the gliding of his hands, Ino continued.

"...If the *Holy Shrine Maiden hadn't challenged you*—what did you plan to do?"

—That was the one unresolved question still hanging on the old Werebeast's mind. However cornered they might have been, he couldn't fathom the Shrine Maiden initiating a challenge so easily.

—*Learn as much as you can from that amusing lot. 'The way of the weak' and all.* Through the back of Ino's mind flitted the Shrine Maiden's words. Indeed, he had been shown that "way so no one would die" that Sora had confided to Izuna. However, Ino was neither so unskilled that he could accept such improbable perspicuity blindly nor, unfortunately, so skilled as the Shrine Maiden, who could see the Immanity's true purpose completely. But Sora answered his question casually.

"In that case—we probably would have rolled out our extraspecial ultimate troll."

Namely—

"—We would have *actually* told Elven Gard and Avant Heim the details of the game."

—At this revelation, Ino couldn't hide his wince.

"We've got Chlammy in Elven Gard and Jibril in Avant Heim. We just tell them, 'Give it to us,' and we'll probably *get it back*. That said, it would cause some significant damage to the Eastern Union, so we didn't want to do it that way."

Plus—he continued…

"—The Shrine Maiden *could probably see that coming*, and that's why she got on board."

—Yes, to the Shrine Maiden, who had supposed Sora and Shiro to be agents of Elven Gard, that must have seemed the worst conceivable outcome. And that was why, *before that happened*, she'd have to grab the territory to fight back…or she'd be trapped, she must have figured.

"Hey, Gramps, you know what 'checkmate' means?

"It's not like *shogi* where you only say 'check' as a warning—'checkmate' is an *announcement* you've won."

Forming a humongous smile that drained the blood from one's face…

"When I met you for the first time, I told you that anything you did would be useless, *didn't I*?"

Through the back of Ino's mind flitted Sora's prediction that day he bet the Immanity Piece.

"I said—'check*mate*.' "

—Yes, by that day. Everything was already over.

(—O Holy Shrine Maiden, do you tell me to trust this man?) It could indeed be said that this Immanity made a decision to our benefit. But to be outstripped so easily, so spectacularly—(Does it not mean…that we may be *stabbed in the back* at any time…?) While Ino was thus preoccupied with doubt, Sora changed up the pace and dropped his serious face, saying to the bunny-girl he'd been stroking the whole time:

"Welll then, I hate to say it, but it's time I go look for a place to sleep tonight!"

"…See you, later…bunny-*chan*…"

And so Sora, casting a sidelong glance at the bunny-girl strolling away while looking back at Sora and Shiro as if she really hated to go, turned his attention to the matter at hand.

"Okay, Izzy, for now we gotta set up our fort. You know where we can stay around here?"

"...? Why don't you just stay at my place, dumbass, please?"

"...The sleepover, event...woot..."

"Izuna's house must be loaded with games! Amirite?!"

"No shit, please. So you'll take me on, please?"

"Of course! So first, let's play games all night, and then in the morning, let's go back into town! Oh, Izzy...if this country has video games, does that mean there's also porn—?"

"...Brother..."

"What! What possible problem could there be with me playing them secretly?"

As the three bickered, one who'd been observing from a slight remove now wove her way through Jibril and Ino—

"I—I finally caught up to you! Y-you two...just what do you think it's like to have a country with no—"

Though the first in pursuit, Steph had been left in the dust by everyone, only now breathlessly catching up.

"Jibril! Take Steph and fly to Elkia! Then come back!"

"As you wish."

Jibril grabbed Steph's shoulder lightly. Steph, certain she'd be able to resist the Flügel taking her by force, paled.

"Oh, take Gramps while you're at it! It would probably be tough for Steph alone."

This time it was Ino's face that paled.

"Wha—? D-do you mean I shall have to endure that noise again?!"

"Excuse me, but that's not even the issue! Hey—what—this must be a joke...this—"

"Well then, you two, I shall escort you to the Elkia Royal Castle!"

Jibril made her exodus, leaving only this "tweet" in her wake and the wind that stirred filling the void created by the sudden absence of large masses. This breeze hitting him, Sora sighed— *Hff*—and muttered as if truly tired.

"...God's not gonna smite us for taking a little break, is He?"

Shiro nodded in agreement. *Oookay,* Sora prepped himself.

"So, why don't we enjoy the animal-eared paradise for a bit?!"

——......Steph and Ino, deposited within the Elkia Royal Castle.

...With too many different things to think about, Steph abandoned thinking about anything. In the back of her mind, Sora's words surfaced.

"No one will die... Just a *game.*"

Chewing over statements that in the past had made her doubt the man's sanity, Steph perceived a glimpse of something radical at the edge of her consciousness. If you conquered this world... They must have been misunderstanding something. Having seen the Eastern Union swallowed up without any actual damage, she considered.

—Could it be, of all things, that they intend to take over the world *bloodlessly.* To bring all the races—*into a single harmony against the God*?

...The Tenth of the Ten Covenants.

—Let's all have fun together!—

"Th-that piece of shit—! No, the man who ordered her, too—! Next time you show your face, you'd better be ready, asshole!"

Glancing a Ino beside her, writhing and holding his ears, Steph muttered softly.

"...You'll get used to it."

Apparently finding some kind of special meaning or comfort in Steph's reassurances, Ino followed the girl's lead in slumping to the castle floor, remarking:

"We have our work cut out for us, don't we, Miss Stephanie?"

"...That we do, and that we shall, Mr. Ino."

No one knew that at that very time and place, the Society for Victims of Sora and Shiro was in the midst of being quietly established...

TRUE END

"Ha-choo!"

"Why, Chlammy, how sweet your sneeze sounds. Is someone *talking* about you?"

"...Must you read so much into a simple sneeze?"

—The outskirts of the capital of Elven Gard. Having completed her round of reports without issue, Fi had returned. And Chlammy snapped her fingers before Fi's eyes. What Sora had built into the covenant—the fraudulent accounting of the game. And—*the cancel signal.*

"...My goodness. Why, I was just effectively forced into falsely reporting the rules so that Elven Gard would *lose*."

With a little smile, Chlammy started walking. Fi following along behind.

"Fi, had you *read this far*?"

"Hee-hee. To my chagrin, why, I found myself unable."

She had read as far as Sora using Elven Gard to lay siege to the Eastern Union, but—

"This must be what is called *using up* someone... Why, I was exploited to the very *depths* of my potential..."

Everything that could be had been wrung from Fi and Chlammy, to the extent it was somehow refreshing. Considering this, Chlammy walked quietly. Having touched entirely upon Sora's memories and awareness, Chlammy—like Shiro and like the Shrine Maiden—was one of the few parties in the world who entirely grasped Sora's plan, his imagined *method to beat the game*. On the map of that strategy—her own name was engraved clearly.

—Annotated with a brief and preposterous statement of her mission. But even faced with such a chore, Chlammy evinced no despair, no unease. With all those memories now filtered through the match with the Eastern Union, there was one thing Chlammy recalled. In the tournaments to decide the monarch of Elkia—his words as he'd grabbed her chin and fixed her with his gaze.

—Don't—underestimate humans like that.

Having been witness to the potential of humans before her eyes, she'd spoken of the limits of Immanity. She laughed at herself.

—She—was an Immanity, too.

"It's not my imagination, is it…? Why, Chlammy, you've changed a bit."

"Perhaps it is the influence of that man's memories. You object?"

"Hmmm, I only regret I may no longer be able to see the crybaby Chlammy."

"How many times do I have to tell you I don't cry?!"

But then Fi cautioned seriously.

"But, Chlammy? Even if you try to be like that man—Sora—"

"I know. I don't have the foundation of his confidence—Shiro."

Yes, even Sora, who could pull off such feats. Without Shiro, his absolute, he couldn't even remain confident about himself.

"But I have you, Fi. I'll find my own way."

A way for the weak, as the weak, to take down the strong. A way for herself, as herself, to overcome her own limits.

—A way to fly without being able to fly—she'd find it. Just a little humbled, Chlammy turned to face Fi again.

"…Will you help me?"

"Why, of couurse I will. For you, Chlammy, I'd make enemies of the whole worrld."

Fi grasping Chlammy's hand and smiling like the sun. Chlammy nodding gently and walking once more.

"In that case…let us go, Fi."

"Why, certainly!"

Hff, Chlammy subtly sighed.

"*Undermine Elven Gard from within*—it's easy for him to say, isn't it?"

She faced the grandiose mission assigned to her by Sora, yet no unease remained on her face. Her feet as they moved forward held only deliberate purpose.

"Very well, why don't I go ahead and do it for him? Just you wait—Sora."

Her face as she continued onward bore the expression of a contender.

A way for humans—as humans—to surpass humanity, to surpass the Ixseed—even to surpass the God. This was what the two sought as they walked forward. A means for Chlammy and Fi to create their own wings, of their own design. The two shadows headed beyond the horizon—but first—

 AFTERWORD

Here comes Christmas once agaiin! To collect the strain of leisure time that once was fuun!

...This is Yuu Kamiya, back after four months with seasonal gags that will have expired by the time this goes on sale. This volume, as I mentioned in the afterword to the second, is a volume of convergence that brings together the currents flowing from the first volume so that the preparations Sora and Shiro have been plotting for "beating the game" all come into place. Basically, it's a turning point that wraps up an arc, and given that—it's frightfully dense and heavy... For this reason, I'm thinking I want to make the next volume wonderfully fluffy and light. You know, Sora and Shiro decide to hang around in the Eastern Union for a while, take in the animal ears, and hey, it's a maritime nation—of course it's got beaches. There'll be *Eek! Tee-hee-hee!* developments in the swimsuit episode, and Sora will come to an epiphany: *who the hell cares about work? I'm gonna live in* moe-moe *land!* (Yeah, I know no one says *moe-moe* anymore—)

"You'll get lost if you start scribbling out your real-life wishes in your work. ♥"

—Wh-who the hell are you?! What did you do with my usual editor, Editor S for Sadist!

"S for Sadist—*switched jobs.*"

...What are you saying? You sound like certain cicadas when they cry! You didn't—

"From this volume on, I, 'S the Second,' will be your editor. Looking forward to it. ♥"

Oh, but now my editor is a woman with a sweet-sounding voice. Maybe she'll treat me—

"So, Mr. Kamiya, when can we expect the *twenty pages of color illustrations* we ordered?"

—If you'd only give me time for a brief vision of fancy. I have now decided to call you Editor S for Sadist the Second.

"Hee-hee, you may call me whatever you like, as long as the manuscript gets in. ♥"

...Uh, uhh...I-I'm sorry. All my time got eaten up by the main text, and now that I'm writing this, the situation with the illustrations is pretty bad. I should particularly note that I don't really understand where it says here, "Manga launch"... I sort of failed to notice it, which is what I said to myself so I could blatantly ignore it. It's not really—

"Oh, don't worry. We hired someone else to do the manga."

You, wh-what, seriously? Thank—

"Yes, an artist by the name of **Mashiro Hiiragi**?"

That's my damn wife!!

"So you're going to be on the first page of *Alive* coming out the same month. Cheers. ♥"

Hey—d00d, did you really take all that BS from the last volume—?

ZEE (CHHH)
ゼ
HAA (CHFF)
は
W-WE PULLED IT OFF-
DOOD.
Brother—Sora, 18: Virgin, awkward, loser, game veg
MY SISTER! WHEN CONTROLLING THE "MAIN" ACCOUNT—
—COULD YOU REFRAIN FROM USING YOUR FEET?!
YOUR BROTHER'S POOR HEART!
GOT, NGRY.
Sister—Shiro, 11: Truant, awkward, shut-in, game veg
ZUZU (SLRRP)
ZUZU (SLRRP)
...WANT, SOME?
FOOD
CALORIEMATE (POTATO)

"...is what it looks like! As Mr. Kamiya was unable to condense the main text, we were only able to fit in one page, but we hope you'll pick up *Comic Alive*. ♥"

Well, the song and dance aside. As I suppose you can see, I'm also helping out on it. And by "helping out" I mean **doing everything up to the sketches**. Since it's a joint project with my wife, I guess it's all right, but...

"Mm? We got your proper authorization, didn't wee?"

I would say drawing my wife over to your side using the bait "I'll give you some tofu skin" (TRUE STORY), going over the plan past the point of no return, and then telling me about it, all while calling that "proper authorization" is a fine example of a crime against humanity, don't you think?!

"Oh, well, you see, when I took over from the previous editor, he told me—"

Mr. Kamiya plays mind games in real life, too, so don't give him the upper hand.

"—so I figured basic tactics would dictate I *undermine your position and cut off your escape*, right? ♥"

* * *

——......

...*Hff*, so, yeah, there's the manuscript for the fourth volume, and there's the manga and the illustrations. So now, basically, I have no choice but to work like a pack horse, do I? Time for me to fulfill my duty as one of the cogs that make up the social—

"Wow, Mr. Kamiya, now you're talking! That's the spirit!"

What—you've never heard of sarcasm?! W-well, anyway, see you in the next volume! Ciao!

NOTE: THE AUTHOR IS SCRATCHING OUT THIS PREVIEW ON THE MOMENTUM OF HIS ALL-NIGHTER BEFORE THE DEADLINE (CAN'T TAKE NO MORE)
パパ♥
DADDY <3
…あ？
...WTF?
IXSEED RANK 15: SIREN
NO GAME NO LIFE, VOLUME 4 (WORKING TITLE)
I GUESS THE BROTHER'S EXPERIENCED VIRGIN INSEMINATION OR SOMETHING (WORKING SUBTITLE)
OUT, WELL, YOU KNOW, SOON, PROBABLY, OR SOMETHING (WHO KNOWS)

A BARRAGE OF BATTLES AGAINST STRONGER RACES HAS EXHAUSTED THE ~~AUTHOR~~ " "!!
SPIR*IT
FWSHHH
AS, AFFLICTED BY BURNOUT SYNDROME, THE TWO ANNOUNCE THEIR INTENT TO LANGUISH IN THE EASTERN UNION...
...WILL STEPH, ENTRUSTED WILLY-NILLY WITH THE FOUNDATION OF AN UNPRECEDENTED COMMONWEALTH AFTER ABSORBING THE WORLD'S THIRD-LARGEST COUNTRY...EVEN WANT TO SAVE THEM?!

HAVE YOU BEEN TURNED ON TO LIGHT NOVELS YET?

IN STORES NOW!

SWORD ART ONLINE, VOL. 1–5
SWORD ART ONLINE, PROGRESSIVE 1–3

The chart-topping light novel series that spawned the explosively popular anime and manga adaptations!

MANGA ADAPTATION AVAILABLE NOW!

ACCEL WORLD, VOL. 1–4

Prepare to accelerate with an action-packed cyber-thriller from the bestselling author of *Sword Art Online*.

MANGA ADAPTATION AVAILABLE NOW!

REKI KAWAHARA
ILLUSTRATION BY HIMA

SPICE AND WOLF, VOL. 1–15

A disgruntled goddess joins a traveling merchant in this light novel series that inspired the *New York Times* bestselling manga.

MANGA ADAPTATION AVAILABLE NOW!